A Changed Reflection

Ashley Wylder

Copyright © 2017 Ashley Wylder
All rights reserved
First Edition

PAGE PUBLISHING, INC.
New York, NY

First originally published by Page Publishing, Inc. 2017

ISBN 978-1-63568-974-7 (Paperback)
ISBN 978-1-63568-975-4 (Digital)

Printed in the United States of America

At times our own light goes out
and is rekindled by a spark from
another person.
Each one of us should pause and
feel deep gratitude for those who
have lighted the flame
within us.
Thanks to a special friend for
rekindling the spark.
You brought Ashley Wylder to life!

Chapter One

Tess could feel the warmth on her face. She slowly eased her arms from under the covers and stretched them upward as if she were trying to reach for the heavens. She gazed out the bedroom window. The sun's rays peeked out between the trees, welcoming the glorious morning. It was going to be a beautiful day. A slight grin appeared on her face as she breathed in the lake air. She pushed back the covers and scrunched them down to the bottom of the bed with her feet. It was time to rise and shine.

She once again stretched her arms to the ceiling and then very slowly extended them outward and let them fall to her sides. She inhaled deeply. Something told her this day was going to be special. Carrington intuition. She carefully pulled up the covers and made the bed as her mother had taught her. She headed to the other side of the bed and repeated the process. She reached for the decorator pillows and hugged them each gently as she placed them just so on the bed. Her mother had made them and with each hug she felt her mother's presence.

She gazed out the window facing the lake. The pink in the clouds reflected in the water. The lake was smooth as glass. It would be a perfect time for a fast boat ride across the lake with the wind blowing in her face. Maybe if she got her work done, she would treat herself to a ride if the lake was still smooth. It was still early in the season, and not many boats would be out even if it were later in the day.

Why was it that the fabulous days were so often filled with work? She longed to read a book in her nook by the water or let the sun warm her back while riding her bike around the lake. *Oh well, enough daydreaming,* she thought as she turned away from the window. She knew in her heart that there would be more of these precious moments. Her mother would make sure of that.

She would just have to catch some rays washing windows, weeding, and watering her flowers. She headed to the bathroom, and when she returned, she rummaged through her dresser drawer. She found some cute black shorts with small fuchsia flowers on them and a sleeveless fuchsia button-down shirt to match. If she had to work, she might as well look good doing it. She buttoned the last button and then paused to look at her reflection in the mirror. The mirror reflected an uncertain face—one with worry lines yet a spark of hope in her eyes. She sighed and headed downstairs to the kitchen.

She grabbed the teakettle from the stove and filled it with water. Once filled, she returned it to the stove, turning on the burner. While she waited, she gazed out the windows toward the lake. She knew it would be easier to put a cup of water in the microwave, but there was something about the teakettle getting all hot and blowing off steam that soothed her.

She cranked open the windows. She welcomed the gentle breeze that touched her face and almost forgot what was ahead of her that morning. The kettle whistled, and she returned to the kitchen to pour the hot water into her cup and wait for her tea to steep. Minutes later she was sipping on Lady Grey and watching the ducks on the water. How lucky she was to have such an amazing view outside her dining room windows. "This is truly my happy place," she thought out loud.

The voice was in her head. *Enough dreaming. Time to get busy. The weeds won't pull themselves.* She set her empty cup in the sink and sighed. She headed outdoors, stopping long enough to grab her phone and earbuds. She had created a station on Pandora featuring the music from the '70s. It brought back many happy memories, along with the stinging, sad ones.

If it doesn't kill you, it makes you stronger, she mused. She was still learning to deal with mistakes from her past. She could live without many things, but music was not one of them. She could get lost in the music in her own world. She knew it well. No one could take those moments away from her.

Tess started the painstaking task of removing the small weeds from the flower bed. She became immersed in her task. She thought of the needlepoint saying that had hung above grandmother's bed that now hung above hers.

When a job is once begun, never leave it till it's done. Be the labor great or small, do it well or not at all. She smiled. A needlepoint that had been passed down through generations from her great-great-grandmother. The one her family had said she and Cat had taken after. The woman who had loved the sea. A strong and resilient woman. Mary Elizabeth Carrington.

The late morning sun rose higher in the sky. She found herself singing along with The Guess Who. "*No time left for you… on my way to better things…*" She heard a noise in the distance, and she paused and looked up. A motorcycle was cruising around the point. *What a great day for a ride,* she thought as she went back to pulling weeds. A bead of sweat trickled down her neck. It was getting hot.

The motorcycle started to slow, and she smiled. So many people slowed down as they passed the house. It had kept its charm from a bygone era. Her mother had made sure of that. The rider didn't keep going; he pulled onto the gravel by the guesthouse. Most likely he probably needed directions.

Damn, she thought. Kool and the Gang was now playing "Celebration." Maybe it would be a quick question. "*What's your pleasure…,*" she hummed as she took off her gardening gloves. "*We're going to have a good time tonight…,*" she continued to hum. Then she stopped dead in her tracks. The earbud she was taking out of her ear dropped out of her hand.

The rider had gotten off his bike and taken off his helmet. Tess stood frozen with her mouth wide open. It couldn't be. How long had it been since she had actually seen him? Three years had passed, and then she had only briefly spoken to him in a crowded room. So many years before that! They had reconnected on Facebook and had exchanged lively banter through texts, but she hadn't seen him face-to-face or spoken to him. Somehow the years faded.

THAT night became vivid in her mind. But perhaps he didn't even remember. Those memories had led to some amazing dreams for her. But even if he did remember, she certainly didn't look like she had those many years before. She was suddenly aware of the droplets of perspiration running down between her breasts. She took a deep breath and regained her composure.

She smiled and asked with a slight squeak in her voice, "Hey, stranger, what brings you down this way?" The day had become hot, but suddenly she had goose bumps. "I'd give you a hug, but I'm all hot and sweaty." She giggled nervously. She waited for his response, not knowing what direction it would take.

"You're not getting off that easily! As I recall, you gave some of the best hugs around. Besides, I like a hot woman, so come here and refresh my memory." He laughed as he held out his arms.

Oh my, she thought and felt a tingling through her body as she knew this type of banter from his texts. Her heart skipped a beat as she walked over to where he was standing. He gently pulled her close. His body was warm. She felt herself melting into his strong arms. She had dreamed of this often. The years melted away. And then the moment was over.

She felt flushed. "So I didn't give you a chance to answer. What brings you to my neck of the woods?" An impish grin appeared on her face. Two could play this game.

"I texted you I would stop sometime when I was down this direction. I was heading south, and you popped into my head, and here I am. Memories run deep, Tess." He winked at her and smiled.

"I'll accept that," she said. "Hey, I bet you're hot and thirsty from your long ride. Come on in and I'll get you something cold to drink."

"You're the hot one," he chuckled with a smile on his face. "Always have been. Show me the way to your kitchen, and I'll fix a cold one for you." The smile remained on his face.

"Follow me," she replied. He still made her heart quiver. She turned around and headed to the screen door, holding it open until he grabbed it. "Nice house," he commented as they passed through the spa room into the kitchen.

"Thanks. This was so my mom's house. It's ironic because my dad passed on his love of the water but he never wanted to leave the farm. I was afraid he would sell it after Mom died, but I let him know how much it meant to me. So he promised not to sell it if I took care of it. It's a lot of work, but it's my little piece of heaven."

Greg eyed the refrigerator and opened the door and quickly scanned the contents. "I think we could both use a good cold beer." He grabbed the beers and took one and held it to her neck. Chills ran down her spine, and she shivered. "Did that cool you off?" he said with a smile. Her heart was racing. He still knew how to push her buttons.

"Come, I'll show you the house," she said, trying to find a distraction to the feelings that were stirring inside her. She turned away but could feel his hot breath on her neck. He was following very closely behind her. She stopped and turned to ask him a question and found her face in his chest. She had forgotten how tall he was.

Before the words could come out, he was leaning over and kissing her lips softly. "Sorry, I've been wanting to do that for a long time," he said with a strangeness in his voice. He felt her body quiver.

"That's okay," she said in a voice barely above a whisper. She tried to act like it was just a casual kiss. It was anything but, and her body was gasping for breath. She felt her nipples get hard. *Breathe*, she told herself. She couldn't let herself go there.

"Let's drink our beers out on the porch, and then I'll show you the rest of the house," she said. "We have a lot to catch up on." Her head was spinning. She led him to the porch. She settled on the couch facing the lake, and he sat down next to her.

"Great view. Is this where you see all those great sunsets you post?" he asked. "I like this room. It feels real homey."

"Thanks. It is a great view, isn't it? I love the fact that you can look out across the lake and see trees and not houses. That will never change. It's really cool to watch a rainstorm come across the lake. It's a wall of water. When you see it coming, you have about four minutes to get everything closed up."

She was babbling. Why was she so nervous? He was just a friend from high school. She was sure he had no idea that she had been hot for him. During all the months she and Todd had been broken up during high school, she had wished he would have asked her out. She loved watching him play football. She had been a cheerleader and had a front-row view. If only…

"How's the fishing here?" he asked.

She knew he liked to fish from the pictures he had posted. She turned and looked at him to answer and realized he had been studying her face. What was it he was seeing?

"It's great. This is one of the prime spots on the lake. I don't really fish. I just eat it. Someone else has to catch it and clean it. I don't like to touch the worms," she replied as she scrunched her face as she thought of the squirmy, slimy creatures.

He laughed. "A good farm girl like you? I thought you probably played in the dirt and made mud pies growing up. You never picked up all the worms after a rainstorm?"

She shook her head with a slightly grossed-out look on her face.

"I'm surprised, Tess. So are you a hunter?"

"No. My dad doesn't like guns. I've never even held one. Although it has crossed my mind that I might need to get one. So do you like to hunt, Greg?"

He nodded at her with a smile.

"Well then. Maybe you could take me hunting and show me the ropes. But you'd have to be patient with me. I'm a virgin hunter," she teased. Her heart was racing. She smiled. Even during their lively banter through texting, he made her heart race.

"I could certainly take care of that without a problem." A smile slowly appeared on his face as if he were remembering something. "Same old Tess. You're still a tease." He laughed. "I promise I'll be gentle," he said as his hand softly touched her face.

"Ha!" she chortled as she hopped off the couch. *Refocus*, she thought to herself. She could still feel that electricity between them she had felt years before. "I'll grab us another beer. Are you hungry?"

"Yeah, but not for anything in your refrigerator," he said as he winked at her with a smile. That smile. The smile that drove her crazy back in high school. The smile that still made her heart skip a beat. Some women loved a man in a suit. She loved a man with a great smile.

"You haven't changed a bit! If I didn't know better I'd say you were trying to get me drunk." She giggled. She always found herself giggling when she got nervous. It had been years since she felt butterflies in her stomach. It was a feeling that had become buried in years of nothingness. She thought it had been lost forever.

"Maybe. I might get lucky." He grinned. She felt herself losing control. Where were these feelings coming from? She had to get a grip on herself. She was glad she was facing away from him as she was leaving the room. She felt the blood rush to her face.

Change the subject, she thought. *Regroup and focus*. "So, Greg, remind me. What brings you down this way?" She knew he had told her, but she needed something to take her away from where her mind was heading.

"I've texted you a couple times that I might stop sometime to see your place. I was on my way south, and my bike decided to take a little detour!" he hollered from the other room. "I had to see the place that makes you so happy. I figured it had to be special. And from everything I've seen so far, it certainly is."

"I'm glad. I haven't seen you in a long time, and it certainly is a nice surprise. It's good to actually talk to you in person. I remember when some of us got together a couple years ago. And before that…" her voice trailed off.

It was THAT night. Sometimes she thought she just imagined it. It was a magical night to her. That one special night that haunted her dreams. She had forgotten so many memories from her past, but this one was etched in stone. He probably didn't even remember. She handed him the beer and then sat down beside him. He leaned over and whispered in her ear. "You mean that night I took you home after the party at the club?"

She felt the blood rush to her face. Oh my god. He had remembered. But what exactly did he remember? "That was a great party. I had fun," she tried to say nonchalantly.

"That wasn't what was great," he replied with a mischievous smile forming on his face as he looked directly into her eyes.

"So just what was so great about it, then?" she challenged him as she looked directly back into his eyes. She needed to know just what he remembered. Were there emotions involved besides hers? She felt her cheeks get hot. The question had been asked. Did she really want the answer?

He reached over and placed his hand on her inner thigh and gently squeezed. "I can still remember you lying naked on my bed. It was one of the most beautiful sights I've ever seen." She let out a little gasp. All these years. That night meant something to him too. It hadn't just been a one-night stand. If she had only known. But she couldn't go there. Not now.

"Well, I'm sorry to say I don't look like that anymore." She grabbed his hand, stood up, and pulled him off the couch. She could feel the heat from his body. She pulled away slightly. "Hey, let me show you the rest of the house."

He pulled her close again. He gently grabbed her chin and looked directly into her eyes. "Let me be the judge of that." He leaned down and kissed her lips tenderly.

She nervously giggled and pulled away. Her heart was beating a hundred beats a minute. Her head was whirling. It was too much too fast. For years she had thought of him and that night. That magical night for her. High school was something she tried to forget, but she never forgot him. Her mind started to drift back in time.

She thought of the night she climbed out the window onto the second floor porch of their farmhouse. She had signed up for basketball cheerleader tryouts. Her boyfriend Todd told her no. He didn't play basketball and couldn't keep a watchful eye on her. He controlled her, and she did what he told her. If she jumped from the porch and broke her leg, she couldn't try out.

She didn't jump but had to endure the humiliation of telling the coach she couldn't try out. She was too afraid to face the wrath of Todd if she didn't say no. He had told her to quit all the activities she loved, and she did what he had told her. She had faced his anger—it wasn't a pretty thing. But their passion certainly was.

Over and over whenever they would break up, Todd had told her she was a liar and a loser. He told her that no one else would love her. She believed him. There was no one else to tell her otherwise. She thought a bad relationship was better than no relationship.

During those painful times, she had watched Greg and wished he would come save her. Number 18. A football letterman. Her secret prince charming. He would take her away from the hurt and provide her the kind and tender passion she so desperately craved.

But she had that ONE night. And he remembered. Oh my god. Now what would she do? But that was years ago, and she had changed. But the feelings had never totally gone away. They would keep popping up in her mind at the strangest times. Should she just hold on to her memories? Things were complicated. Did she want to go there?

Greg touched her face gently. "Hey, Tess, where are you?" he asked. "Did you take a trip down memory lane?" His touch brought her back to the moment.

Chapter Two

She hung up the phone as tears rolled down her cheeks. Tess wondered if high school was this hard for everyone. Did she really deserve to be treated like this? Todd had broken up with her again. It was the day after Thanksgiving. With her luck, it would stay this way until after Valentine's Day. How convenient her birthday was just days before Valentine's Day. He wouldn't have to give her a thing!

Now he would do whatever he wanted. She would be left alone and lonely. No one else would have anything to do with her. He would make sure of that. It wasn't the first time he had done this. She would wait for him to come back. She always did. A bad relationship was better than no relationship.

She sighed. She searched her mind and wondered when it had gotten so bad. She closed her eyes and tried to remember the feeling of the sun on her face and her ponytail bouncing on her back as they would gallop their horses down the gravel roads. Then they would stop and find a place to rest the horses and embrace each other. He had stolen his first kiss under the giant oak at the deserted farm and had made her heart melt. He had caused her body to feel things she didn't quite understand but couldn't get enough of. His eyes were the color of the clear-blue sky. He took her breath away. Those carefree sunny afternoons of horseback riding seemed like ancient history. Yet she kept holding on, thinking that somehow she might find that happiness again. She was the eternal optimist.

She opened the refrigerator and grabbed an apple. Some days she wished it were the poison apple like the one Snow White ate. And the cute boy who always smiled at her in homeroom would kiss her and take her away from the unhappiness. She looked further, but it was the only thing that vaguely interested her. She could eat it slowly and make it last. It will fill her up. She was glad her parents were gone for the evening. She didn't want to listen to her mother discuss her eating habits or lack thereof. She grabbed her books from the kitchen table.

She climbed the stairs to her bedroom. It was the only place she could be her real self. She put her books on her desk and took her jacket off and grabbed a hanger. She carefully hung the jacket in her closet. She was proud of her home economics project. Sewing a jacket that had nineteen pattern pieces out of corduroy was no easy task. She had gotten an A on her project. At least there was something she could do right.

Then she saw it. The royal-blue velvet dress. She ran her hands across the inset lace. She could feel herself get angry. Rick Steiner had asked her to his company Christmas party the year before. Todd had broken up with her because she had gone out with friends when he had instructed her not to. It was always a control issue. Rick had asked her, and she had said yes. She was so excited for the party. She liked Rick. He was cute and had a wonderful smile. She had spent hours making that dress. It was beautiful, and it made her feel special. The day before the party Rick called and told her he couldn't take her. She was devastated.

She later found out why. Todd had found out that Rick had asked her to the party. He had tailed Rick in his car as he was on his way home from work. When he finally caught up with him, Todd made it clear that he would beat the shit out of him if he took her to the party. Todd was known for his temper, and Rick wasn't a tough guy. Rick felt he had no choice. She was left with heartache.

So Todd didn't want her, but he made sure no one else would want her either. Why did she always wait for him to come back? Why wasn't she strong enough to tell him to go to hell and leave her alone for good? She knew why. It was about the passion. The addictive intense emotion that controlled her. A desire he fulfilled. And he made her believe that she couldn't find it anywhere else.

She sat down at her desk to finish her poem for English class. She wrote from her heart. Her journal was filled with writings of her heart. It was her coping mechanism. She hoped her teacher liked it. Another person to please. At least she had school to focus on. It was something she excelled at that he couldn't control. She read the poem out loud to herself one last time. Each time she read it, it filled her with great sadness.

> It's hard to go on
> When the mirror only reflects
> An inanimate object.
> Something that has no feelings,
> No love, no understanding.
> And it hurts me to know
> That reflection is me.

This was the reflection she saw in the mirror. A reflection that brought tears to her eyes. She hoped maybe her poem was just good enough to be chosen for the biannual anthology of high school poetry. And just maybe, when her teacher was reading it, he would see she was reaching out, that she needed help. "Why doesn't anyone see?" she asked herself.

She looked out the window onto the yard and into the field across the road. The moon was almost full and brilliant. It created hauntingly beautiful shadows across her carpet. She sighed. Now she would spend another holiday season alone. Her room had become her best friend. Todd had threatened her every time she talked to anyone other than him so that people thought she had no interest in them. She had heard people talking in the halls. No one would call her.

Maybe she would work up the courage to go to the basketball game the next night. She knew Todd wouldn't be there and maybe she could have a little fun. She deserved at least that. She had the night to think about it. She slowly peeled away the layers of her clothes until there was nothing left but her skin. She loved the way being naked felt. It made her feel free. She quietly opened her dresser drawer and reached underneath the neatly folded sweaters where she had carefully hidden her pink lace baby doll nightie and slipped it over her head. What a waste no one would see how good it looked on her. Lace made her feel special.

She shuffled through her albums. How lucky she was to have her brother's old stereo system and albums. If only he hadn't gone so far away to college. He would have taken care of the Todd situation. He had always looked out for her. She carefully took *The Association's Greatest Hits* from its cover and placed it on the spindle of the stereo. The arm clicked, and the album dropped to the turntable. She looked into the mirror of the vanity as the room filled with the melancholy words of "Cherish." The reflection of the girl in the mirror had tears in her eyes.

She took a deep sigh and walked over to her door and turned off the lights. The light of the moon continued to create shadows through her window. She crawled into her bed and snuggled under the covers. She fluffed the pillow under her head and pressed her fingertips on the back of her neck to release the tension. She slowly slid them around her neck and down the front of her chest until she reached her breasts. She slid her hands underneath her nightie. She closed her eyes and caressed her nipples until they grew hard. She concentrated on the sensations she felt.

Then slowly she slid one hand down her body until she felt the moist warmth. She let her fingers explore her body. She found the spot that produced great pleasure and touched herself gently and then more deliberately until her body quietly convulsed. She heaved a heavy sigh as she drifted off as The Association was singing "Never My Love."

The next morning she awoke with the sun streaming into her room. The darkness was gone. It was a new day. She crawled out of bed and grabbed her bathrobe from the closet. She headed to the bathroom and turned on the water. Once it became hot she shed her robe and stepped into the tube and let the water wash her troubles away. She knew her time was limited, so she quickly soaped up and rinsed off. She ripped the towel from the towel bar and dried herself carefully. She wrapped the towel around her and knotted it between her breasts.

She brushed her hair and applied a coat of mascara to her eyelashes. She looked at herself in the mirror and the morning light brought a happier reflection. She grabbed her robe and headed to her room. She threw on some jeans but chose her sweater carefully. It fit snuggly and showed just the right amount of cleavage. Maybe Greg would notice. She smiled at that thought. She headed downstairs.

"Good morning Sunshine." She grinned. Her dad always said that to her every morning. He smiled at her. She was not a morning person. "I bought you some raspberries." He knew they were her favorite.

"Thanks, Dad." He was the only other guy she could count on besides her brother. *If he only knew*, she thought. He was a quiet, kind man. Maybe that was because her mother talked all the time and never let him get a word in edgewise. He was a smart man. She knew her father would never let anyone hurt his daughter. But she was too ashamed to tell him. All she wanted was for him to be proud of her.

She popped the last raspberry in her mouth when she heard her mother holler from the other room. "Come on, let's go. Unless you want to ride the bus." Her mother worked at the school and she got a ride with her every day. Anything was better than riding the bus.

"Coming Mom."

Thank God it was Friday. She didn't have any classes with Todd and maybe she could avoid him altogether. Today she would try hard to be happy during school. She knew deep down that there was a girl inside her that wanted nothing more than to be happy and laugh. Tonight she would muster up the courage to go to the ball game.

She heard the door close ahead of her and grabbed her books and purse. By the time she got to the garage her mother had already backed the car out. She slid in the front seat beside her mom and peered out the window at the cat crossing the yard. Her mother was talking to her but she wasn't listening. She occasionally said "yep" as she tried to give the appearance she was. She had to keep her from asking too many questions. She couldn't deal with that today.

"This door okay?" Her mother had stopped the car at the side door of the school.

A CHANGED REFLECTION

"Perfect. Thanks mom." She liked coming in that door, Greg's locker was down that hall. Maybe she would get a chance to say hi. Her heart raced just thinking about him. His smile made her whole body happy. No such luck today. She tried to hide her disappointment. She headed to algebra class.

She liked algebra. She liked school period. It came easy for her. Her idea of studying for a test meant minutes not hours. It was a good thing because half the time she had no social life and for a good share of the other half Todd had her waiting by the phone that never rang. Homework helped pass the time.

She also liked algebra class because Todd's cousin Scott was in this class and sat by her. She knew deep down she related better to guys and at least she had one guy she thought she could talk to without a problem. Scott was always there for her. He always listened. He had a way of taking the hurt away, if only for a while. He knew his cousin well and he tried to ease the pain he sometimes caused Tess.

She sat down. There were still a few minutes before the bell rang. "Did you see those guys flinging meatballs in the lunch room today?" Scott asked her chuckling.

"Yeah. One flew right over my head." She laughed. "I'm lucky it didn't land in my hair." Some days she forgot what it felt like to laugh. It felt good.

She grabbed her book and opened it to the assignment posted on the black board. Then, for reasons unknown, she glanced out into the hall. If looks could kill. Todd was standing in the hall outside her algebra class. His glare pierced her to the core. A brief happy moment was now replaced with an overwhelming feeling of dread. It didn't matter that they were broken up. Todd would make sure she paid for what he perceived as her indiscretion.

She felt totally defeated. Sometimes she wondered if being in a relationship was worth the price even though she currently wasn't in that relationship. She truly believed there had to be some unwritten "guy code" that was like being type cast for a certain character role. Her role was "Todd's girlfriend," regardless of what was happening between them. She was sure he wasn't spending all HIS time alone, but he could make sure she did.

Then a slight smile crossed her face. The pep rally before the basketball game was the next period. It was a requirement that everyone go. It would be her chance to see Greg. He surely knew by now they were broken up. Just maybe he would ask her if she was going to come watch them play. And she would tell him she would come, especially to watch him. Everyone adored Greg.

The bell rang. Class had started.

Chapter Three

"Tess?"

The sound of a boat on the lake brought her back to the moment. "Sorry." She smiled. "I was just remembering when I used to go down your hallway in school hoping you'd be at your locker."

"Wow. Where did that come from?" he asked, looking puzzled. "I do remember seeing you." He smiled. "You used to wear those low cut tops that drove me wild." She felt herself blush. That was always her intention but she had never known if he had even noticed. And now he was here, alone with her and she could feel her breathing become more rapid.

They passed the stairs as she led him to the living room. "Hey, where do these lead?" he asked with a grin.

He knows exactly where they lead, she thought to herself.

"You told me you'd give me a whole house tour." The grin had turned into a full-fledged smile. "Come on, Tess. Don't be shy now."

"I see you haven't outgrown your orneriness," she mused. He knew she would take this as some type of challenge and she rarely backed down from a challenge. She turned and climbed the stairs. She knew he was checking her out with every step. And with every step the butterflies in her stomach fluttered more. Deep breaths she told herself. He's just flirting with you. On the last step he goosed her and she squealed.

"Hey, no fair," she giggled. She always giggled when she got nervous.

"I just made you squeal like a little pig." He laughed.

"I guess you can't ever take the farm out of the girl," she replied breathlessly.

He noticed and questioned her, "Out of shape?"

"No," she said slowly and in a very controlled voice. She took a long, deep breath. Her body was feeling things she hadn't felt in a very long time.

She took him down the hall to show him the view from the street side. He brushed against her as he headed to the window to take in the view. She knew he had done it on purpose. "Did your mother do all of this?" he asked as he turned from the window.

"Yes," she replied. "She took things from all over and made them work together. She had quite a knack for that." She headed for the door.

"I can see that," he said as he followed her. "She was quite a lady." They passed the bathroom which she pointed out without stopping since it really needed no explanation. "Like her daughter," he added with a smile that melted her heart.

"Yes, she was. I miss her."

"I bet you do," he said tenderly as he grabbed her hand and squeezed it gently. His warm rugged hand dwarfed hers. She took him into the room facing the lake and he immediately was drawn to the window. "Wow, the view is great from here. You almost feel like you're in a treehouse," he remarked as he sat down on the edge of the bed and peered out the window.

She was standing in the middle of the room watching him. His hair had grayed but it made him look distinguished. His skin was tanned. He seemed mesmerized with the view. Without warning he turned around and reached out, grabbed her hand and pulled her in front of him. Tess tried to pull away slightly but he pulled her back.

"I've thought about another moment like this for a very long time," he said quietly as he looked into her eyes. He pulled her closer and used his knees to hold her. Their eyes remained locked. Then very slowly and methodically he unbuttoned her blouse, pausing between each button. With each button she let out a little gasp. His hands grabbed the blouse and gently pushed it off her shoulders. Her blouse fell to the floor.

A CHANGED REFLECTION

His hands cradled her face. She closed her eyes for a moment. His hands were strong and warm. She opened her eyes and saw him studying her face. "You're just as beautiful as I remember," he whispered as his hand stroked her face. Then, without hesitation, he released the clasp on the front of her bra, pushed it aside and drew her close. He nuzzled his face in her breasts and kissed them tenderly.

She knew he felt her quiver and was sure he could hear her heart beating out of her chest. She closed her eyes and savored the moment. "Still absolutely gorgeous Tess." Before she could open her eyes she felt his lips on hers. She opened her eyes and melted into his arms.

Then, while searching her eyes he took her breasts into his hands and gently rolled her nipples between his fingertips. He smiled as they hardened beneath his touch. All the blood was rushing from her head. She felt faint. Then he kissed her on her neck moving ever so slowly toward her breasts. She let out a little gasp as she felt his lips on her nipple. First one side and then the other.

He released his grasp on her. She locked eyes with him as he undid her shorts. He pulled them down around her ankles so she could step out of them. His hands then wandered up her inner thighs and found their way under her panties. Chills ran down her back. He pulled her close to him and kissed her belly.

Every part of her was on fire. He felt the wetness as he removed her panties. He pulled her gently onto the bed and rolled her onto her back. He kissed her on the lips first tenderly and then with more intensity. "Don't move," he whispered. "Just enjoy it."

She closed her eyes as she felt his fingers start at her neck and transverse her body, stopping to tenderly touch her hardened nipples and then weave their way across her belly. She felt herself holding her breath as he reached between her legs. "Breathe," he said as he nibbled on her ear. She exhaled and felt his lips on her breasts.

She squirmed underneath his touch. She tried to close her legs, but he wrapped his leg around hers and held them apart. Slowly and methodically he alternated between rubbing her and slipping his fingers inside her. He watched and smiled as she took pleasure from his touch and her body started to shudder. "Do you like it," he asked in a whisper. She could only smile and nod.

He kissed her neck gently until she could catch her breath. She rolled onto her side and pushed him onto his back and fumbled with the buttons on his shirt. She pulled it off of him and tossed it onto the floor. "Hold me close," she pleaded. He cradled her in his arms and held her close. She loved the way skin on skin felt. *If only this moment could last forever,* she thought.

She rolled off of him and fumbled with his belt buckle and zipper. Could he tell she was as nervous as a schoolgirl? It had been so long but she wanted it so much. He slid off the bed and pulled off his jeans. He lay back down and pulled her close to him again.

She felt his hardness against her leg. He kissed her neck, and it sent chills down her spine. One arm was trapped underneath his body, and with one hand, he grabbed her other arm and held in securely. His free hand found its way between her legs. She squirmed underneath his touch. She tried to close her legs, but he again wrapped his leg around hers and held them apart. He watched and smiled as she took pleasure from his touch. "Tell me you want me," he whispered.

"You know I do. I need to feel you in me." He smiled and slowly rolled on top of her and found his way. She let out a gasp. She wrapped her legs around him. It was almost like her first time. He was so hot and hard inside her. She didn't want it to stop. Then with one final thrust she felt his warmth spread inside her. She pulled him closer and smiled.

After all these years. It was still magic. Slowly her breathing returned to normal. He whispered her name softly into her ear. Her smile widened. She wanted to hear him say her name again. She felt him brush the hair out of her eyes.

"Tess," he said quietly. Then he said her name a little louder. He was still stroking her face. She opened her eyes. He had a worried look on his face.

"What the..."

Where was she? What had really just happened? She wasn't on the bed overlooking the lake. He was still looking at her with genuine concern in his eyes. It took her a moment to get her bearings. She tried to focus. The fan was blowing the hair into her eyes.

"Hey, girl," he spoke softly as a smile started to emerge on his face. "You came back to me."

She was on the couch in the guesthouse. He was sitting next to her tenderly stroking her face. His hands were warm. She reached out for them and he cradled her hands inside his.

"Silly, girl. You must have been weeding too long without water. I tried to give you a hug and you collapsed in my arms. The door was open to this little house, so I carried you in here." He let out a huge sigh of relief. The look of worry left his face. "Are you always so dramatic that you faint in the arms of your lover?" he chuckled.

"Don't worry." He smiled at her. "I didn't take advantage of you." He winked at her. He helped her sit up. "Now how about we get a cold drink?"

Déjà vu.

Chapter Four

Tess was so glad school was out for the summer. The sun beat down on her. She grabbed the cornstalk and took a giant whack. It felt good to swing the corn knife. It was a productive release for her anger. "Good-looking beans if I say so myself," she said out loud. Of course there was no one around to hear her. She was out in the middle of the bean field. It didn't matter. She was used to talking to her surroundings. She found solace in the quiet and the wind whispering through the beans.

These whispers were much kinder than those she knew had gone around school at the end of the year. She couldn't blame them. It was her fault. Why was she so stupid? They could all see—why couldn't she? Maybe it was because she didn't really want to believe it. He was like an addiction she couldn't let go of. She would have to get proof. He couldn't lie his way out then. "Stop, don't go there now," she told herself. Enjoy the beauty of the day.

Tess felt at peace living in the country. She loved the wide open spaces and watching the amazing change of the seasons. Her favorite time was in the early spring just as the corn started to emerge from the ground. The dark desolation of the winter was gone and replaced with new vibrant green life. She loved being a farmer's daughter... the *Beach Boys* knew what that was all about. She smiled as she hummed the song in her head.

This was a sun lover's dream. Where else could she get a good paying job where she could wear short shorts and a red bikini top that hardly covered her? Plus, there was no one hovering over her. She liked working independently. It was something she had learned at an early age. She closed her eyes for a moment and relished the warmth of the sun as it warmed her body. She took a deep breath and sighed.

Her father had told her when her brother had left for college that he wasn't going to hire a high school boy to help. "You can do it," she remembered him saying. It was a way for her father to connect with her. She was thankful her parents taught her to be self-sufficient and a problem solver. There was no time for self-pity in their house. "Suck it up," her mother would say to her.

"Suck it up." Three little words that really conveyed three huge meanings. She knew them by heart. When you were in physical pain, you found help or endured it and dealt with it but you didn't complain. If you were sad or feeling alone, you just put on your big girl panties, put a smile on your face, and worked through it. If you were just exhausted and tired but there was work to be done, you just did it. There were no pity parties in their home. It was not the Carrington way.

That training had come in handy. She kept the walls up around her world. They were tall and deep. If they were up she was safe and no one could see the hurt and loneliness underneath. If she didn't let anyone get too close they couldn't hurt her. She sometimes wished those walls had been up when she started to go out with Todd. He had hurt her and caused her more loneliness than anyone else in her life. Why didn't she stop it? She wanted to stop. She wanted to have a normal life. Why was high school so complicated? Why couldn't she have lots of guy friends? There was so much less drama with them and the teasing with them made her happy. It was fun—wasn't high school supposed to be fun?

With a few more whacks she had reached the end of the row. She set down the corn knife and walked to the edge of the field where her cooler was. She grabbed her thermos and took a swig of water. It was cold and refreshing. She splashed some of the cold water on her face. She looked to the sky as if the answers might appear in the clouds. The answers weren't there but she knew exactly why she couldn't stop. It was the same reason an alcoholic couldn't stop drinking. Her face was filled with sadness and a tear escaped down her cheek.

She had worked up a sweat and beads of perspiration had trickled down between her breasts. Two more trips across the field and she would be done for the day. Her father was actually a real softie when it came to her. She knew she could negotiate just about anything with him. He had agreed if she got up early she could quit by noon. That would be perfect. She could shower and wash her hair and it would be mostly dry by one. She needed to be in the pool parking lot by one.

Today was going to be a fabulous day. Tess had just bought herself a cute purple, pink and white bikini and today would be the perfect day to try it out at the swimming pool. The best part of the equation was that Todd was out of town with his family and that meant she could actually have fun without worrying that she might do or say something wrong—at least according to him. Besides, they were once again on the "outs."

She smiled. Maybe HE would be there. Her heart skipped a beat. She always thought she was being so obvious whenever he was around. Why was it that guys just didn't seem to get it? He was so hot. His smile drove her crazy. To her dismay he always seemed to have a girlfriend whenever she and Todd were broken up. But there had been times when neither of them seemed to be going out with someone. Tess often wondered why he never asked her out. Her "boyfriend" was hardly ever HER boyfriend. He certainly made the rounds when they were on the outs. It never seemed to work both ways. She closed her eyes and sighed.

Well then," she said out loud, "I better get my ass in gear and finish up!" She smiled and started down the row. The possibility of what might transpire at the pool caused her to giggle with delight. Before long she was down to her last four rows. She found herself walking quicker and then, with one last forceful whack, she eliminated the last stalk of corn. *Good therapy for what ails you. Wasn't that the old saying?* she thought.

She grabbed the thermos and headed to the truck. She hopped in and hoped it would start. She crossed her fingers and turned the key in the ignition. Success! She stayed on the edge of the field until she could access the drive to the road. It was a much smoother ride. She headed down the road toward the farm house. She made a conscious effort to drive slower. The last time she had driven fast and almost ended up in the ditch. Gravel roads were such a buzz kill for driving fast. Minutes later she was turning into the drive.

Tess parked the truck in the shade and headed for the house. She could hear her mother humming in the kitchen. Homemade applesauce. She could smell it a mile away! "Yum," she told her mother and she took a long, deep breath to get the full impact of the wonderful aroma. "Do I need to pick more apples for you? I can do that later if you do. Don't forget to put lots of cinnamon in it please."

"Slow down. Catch your breath. I swear your mouth goes a mile a minute," her mother said to her with a laugh. "Yes, I would really appreciate it if you would pick more apples when you get home. Catrina and her dad are coming down for supper and would like some apples too. Maybe you girls can pick them together. You know she looks up to you like a big sister. And I will add extra cinnamon in the sauce only because you asked so nicely," her mother replied with a smile.

Tess ran up the stairs. *No time to waste*, she thought to herself. If she wanted her hair to be mostly dry by the time she got to the pool she would need forty-five minutes. She knew he liked her long golden-brown hair. She had overheard him in the hall talking to one of his friends as she walked by. *That was one of the things he noticed*, she thought.

She stripped out of her clothes and flung them in her rush. She would pick up her mess later. She quickly rinsed off and washed her hair. No time for little pleasures. Maybe she would get that at the pool today. The thought of that possibility made her giggle again. She knew she looked hot in her suit and she hoped he would think so too.

She wrapped a towel on her head to speed up the drying time while she put on her suit and threw some clothes over the top. Five minutes with the hair dryer and she would be good to go. Moments later she grabbed a towel, some undies and a bra and stuffed them in her duffle bag. She bounded down the stairs. "Well you're in a good mood," her mother noticed. "Have fun today."

"I will, Mom," she said halfway out the door. *Trust me, I will,* she thought with a grin on her face.

She hopped in the car, turned on the stereo and headed into town. She knew she had a couple extra minutes to kill so she stopped at the gas station and grabbed some gum. She hopped back into the car and headed toward the pool. She found a parking spot with shade and parked the car. She was just in time. They were opening the doors. She looked around but she didn't see him. Her heart sank. She let out a big sigh. No, wait. There he was getting out of Kevin's car. She caught his eye and he waved from across the parking lot.

"Keep away today," he hollered. "Guys against girls. You game?" The wide grin on his face let her know he meant business today.

"You know it," she hollered back. Things were starting out just perfectly. She grinned. Why did he make her feel so giddy? If only he would think of her as more than a friend. Then it wouldn't matter that Todd had put her "on hold" again. She would have the courage to tell him to stay away if someone else was giving her the time of day. Someday. She signed in and headed to the girls' locker room. She found an empty locker and threw her bag with her clothes into it.

Five minutes later there was a group of kids on the pool deck. She looked around. *Perfect,* she thought. *More guys than girls. Sweet.* The lifeguards were sauntering over to their chairs. Once they were all in position, their whistles blew.

The guys all did their cannonballs and dives into the water. She snickered to herself. It was their way of impressing the girls. She headed to the ladder. The water took her breath away as she slowly entered. She could feel her nipples get hard and her bikini top didn't cover up that fact. The smart thing would have been to dive in, but that would have gotten her hair wet. She needed that flowing in the breeze effect at least until she got dunked.

"Find the water a little chilly?" Greg said to her with a laugh. He could see through her top once it got wet. He was waiting close by the ladder for her but not so close that it appeared obvious to anyone but her. It was all part of the game.

"Shut up," she growled half laughing as she skimmed the water with her hand and splashed him as she headed out into the pool. She at least had to play a little hard to get.

"You're in for it now," he laughed. He dove under the water and swam toward her. The plan was working. She was in for it now. The flowing hair was going to be history. She was going to get dunked. She watched as he swam closer to her. She knew he was going to dunk her. Only what he grabbed wasn't her head.

Chapter Five

Tess took him in the front door. Her dream was etched in her memory, and the thought of déjà vu was too much. She found her breathing coming in short little breaths. "You okay?" he asked. She could hear the concern in his voice. A true friend.

"I will be," she said taking a deep breath. "I think I just need some water." She knew she needed much more than that. Why did her life have to be so complicated and full of drama? She hated drama. She had had enough of that in high school and had vowed to never go down that path again and somehow it always seemed to find her.

"Nice house," he told her looking around. "I can see why you love it here. I see a lot of you here." She smiled. Her mother's house. She was becoming like her mother. That wasn't such a bad thing. Her mother had taught her how to be strong. Like a rock. She taught her to "suck it up." She often remembered the day her mother had told her she was sorry she had taught her that lesson so well. There had been tears in her mother's eyes. She rarely saw her mother show emotion like that. She knew why. She had the marks on her stomach to forever remind her.

They passed the stairs on the way to the kitchen. He said nothing. The dream had been so vivid. They reached the kitchen, and she opened the refrigerator and grabbed the pitcher of lemonade. "Hey, tall man"—she smiled at him—"would you be a dear and get us some glasses?" His body touched hers as he reached for the glasses. She felt her heart skip a beat. After all these years he still set off a spark in her.

"Shorty"—he grinned at her—"why are the cupboards so high?"

"Gotta have the view, silly. My mom had the lower ones taken out so she could see the lake. Much better view don't you think?" She caught him looking down her blouse as he set the glasses on the counter. He towered over her in her bare feet.

"Yes, it's a wonderful view," he snickered. "Spectacular as always." She smacked the side of his leg. She could feel herself blush. She was short on legs but she certainly didn't lack anything in that department.

"So what do you do when tall handsome gentlemen aren't here?"

"I use these," she laughed as she grabbed her long handled pinchers. "They're great for grabbing all kinds of things." She felt herself getting faint again. She needed that cold drink. That might help settle her down. She poured the glasses only partially full, leaving room for the ice.

He reached into the freezer and grabbed some cubes. He filled each glass and then grabbed one more and dropped it into her cleavage. "Oh my god!" she squealed. "You'll pay for that." The ice on her hot body sent chills down her spine. She shuddered.

"That's what I'm hoping." He winked at her and picked up the glasses. "Where to? I'll follow you."

She turned around and headed to the porch. Every house needed a screen porch. This one had special screen like the one at the farm. You could see out but no one could see in, even if you were right at the door. She remembered when her father and she would sit on the porch when solicitors came. They would be very quiet and the peddlers would knock and knock on the door. "Hmmm, guess no one's home," they would say. It was just one of the pranks her father liked to pull. The prankster in her came naturally. He noticed the concerned look on her face. "Are you sure you're okay? You seem a bit distracted."

"I'll be fine. And yes, this is the place. My happy place." He peered out onto the lake. She studied his face. Tanned from the sun and a few wrinkles. Worry lines her mother used to call them. She knew he had had his share of those. Somewhere hidden there was still that sparkle in his sky-blue eyes and his impish grin. It drove her crazy. She loved to see him smile. She had a feeling he didn't do enough of it.

He turned and caught her looking at him intently. He smiled at her. "Everyone needs a happy place." He turned and sat on the couch and she sat down beside him. "So how the hell have you been Tess? It's been years since we've really talked. It's weird because I consider you one of my oldest and dearest friends, but I actually know very little about you."

It was true. They had gone all through school together. They had gone to the same church. Their fathers did business with each other. They never dated but she had secretly always wanted that even after they graduated. It just never happened and then they lost touch.

They connected once after high school. Oh how they connected as she thought back on that night. She found herself smiling.

"Hey, what are you thinking about that makes you have that shit eating grin on that cute little face?" he asked her.

She blushed at the thought but was sure he didn't remember and then that would only burst her bubble. It was her cherished memory.

"Nothing," she said sheepishly. The thought of that night caused her heart to race. Her palms were sweaty. After all the years he still stirred emotions in her that she thought had long been lost. She felt like that silly girl in high school all over again.

"Well"—he paused—"you know I will get it out of you eventually. You always tell me." He smiled at her and gently took her chin in his hand so he could look directly into her eyes. "You always bare your soul to me."

She looked back at him. It was true. Her soul and a whole lot more. What was going on in that head of his? Did HE remember? How could she know? Did she dare ask him? She had to know for sure but how was she going to find out? She was keenly aware of how warm and strong his hand was. Those wonderful big hands.

"Hey, I made some strawberry rhubarb bars last night. Are you interested?" she asked him. She had no idea what foods he liked. But she did know she was a pretty good baker and made awesome bars.

"Well, yeah. Why have you been holding out on me? That combination is heaven," he said eagerly. They had gotten busy with conversation, and she had forgotten her manners. "Not in my house," her mother's voice whispered in her ear. She blushed as she thought about the dream that in no way was holding out on him. She was glad he hadn't seen her face.

She cut the bars and put them on a cut glass plate. She had long ago decided that the lake house was entitled to the finer things of days gone by. No plastic or paper. Cut glass fit the house, and it seemed like it was a way to pay tribute to her mother. She had been known for being a wonderful hostess. Tess stuck the bars in the microwave for just a few seconds. "Activate the grease," as her father would always say. It did bring out the flavors better.

She carried the warmed bars back to the porch. "Mmmmm, smells like you just baked them." He smiled at her. What was it about his smile that set her off? "You never told me you were a baker. Are you also a candlestick maker?" He laughed.

"No," she replied. "And you never asked before." He took a bite and slowly savored the flavor. From the look on his face she could tell he liked them.

The conversation continued. They talked about childhood, college, kids. Everything but that night. It felt good to have someone to share with that understood her past. Someone who understood where she came from. It was odd how many connections they had to each other.

The sun was starting to come through the screens. That meant it was getting late in the day. It would soon be time to say good-bye. There were still so many unanswered questions. Her mind was racing. Before even one question came out, he interrupted her train of thought.

"Hey, I better get going," he said as he got up off the couch. "This has been a great afternoon. We must do this again but not wait so long." Greg grabbed her hand and pulled her up off the couch.

"Yes, we must do it again," she replied. But the afternoon of conversation was not what she was thinking of. It was that night. She smiled at the thought.

"There you go again with that strange smile. What's going on in that cute little head of yours? Are you going to share?" Greg asked.

She buckled. Okay, she would ask him. It was now or never. He was leaving.

"Do you remember that night we hooked up after high school?"

"Oh yeah," he said with a huge smile emerging on his face as if he were remembering the details. "How could I forget? A naked woman lying on my bed. You were the most beautiful thing I had ever seen Tess."

"Well, if you had the chance, would you do it again?" she asked him seriously.

He held her face in his hands and looked deeply into her eyes. "Like Groundhog Day." He smiled. It was the kind of smile that said "I want it more than you know, but we can't go there. Not now. Not today."

They walked in silence to the street side of the house. He leaned over and gently kissed the top of her forehead. "See you later, Tess." Somehow she knew it wasn't the end of that conversation.

Then he turned and walked to his bike. She followed him. Before he could grab his helmet, she held out her arms. "A hug for the road?" He wrapped his arms around her and hugged her tightly. She felt the electricity between them. She was sure he felt it too.

He hopped on his bike, started the engine and revved it a few times. Then he disappeared just as quickly as he had appeared only a few short hours before.

Chapter Six

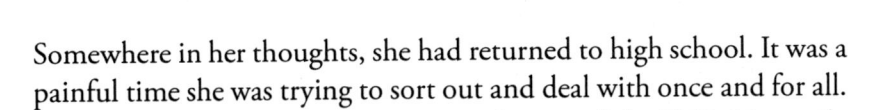

Somewhere in her thoughts, she had returned to high school. It was a painful time she was trying to sort out and deal with once and for all.

"I thought you told me you took care of this?" Todd angrily whispered under his breath and then slammed his locker door. Tears streamed down her cheeks. People were staring. "We'll discuss this later." He stormed off. His words had shredded her being.

Why did she always have to take care of everything? She so wished that just once in a while someone might take care of her. She knew she had done everything right but something must have gone wrong. She didn't know for sure but it didn't look good. How had her world spun so far out of control? She was like a drug addict with a horrible addiction only what she was addicted to wasn't illegal.

She held her head down as she walked through the halls to her next class. She knew he was furious. Damn it. Didn't it take two to create this problem? He wanted it just as much as she did but it had become her fault. It was always her fault. She would be the recipient of his anger later.

She climbed the stairs and headed down the hall to her classroom. She quickly headed in the door and sat down in the first seat by the door. She always sat in the front and by the door. It was easier not to make eye contact with anyone and easier to exit quickly. Safer. She looked at the board for the assignment and the teacher made eye contact with her. "Are you okay, Tess?" Hell no, she wasn't okay, she thought. But she was not about to share what was troubling her.

"I'm fine," she said in a voice barely above a whisper. Then she buried her head in her book. She closed her eyes and tried desperately to keep from getting sick. Her mind drift back to a happier place and time. It wasn't always this way. She remembered her junior high party on the Friday night the last day of school before summer vacation began. She had carefully planned the invitation list. Her beginning as an event specialist.

Her parents had fixed up the basement at the farmhouse and it was the perfect place. Couches, a stereo, no windows and dimmable lights. Her girlfriends had called it the perfect "make out retreat."

Tess had invited everyone she had had classes with. She didn't want hurt feelings. She was delighted when Todd said he would come. They had been science class partners and when his hand had accidentally brushed her arm it left a warm, tingling sensation. She certainly felt the "chemistry" between them. She didn't quite understand what the feeling was but she knew it made her feel good. It was the beginning of a lifelong journey of longing to be touched.

She had worried about the turnout for the party. What if no one came? What about the people she hadn't invited. What if they had gotten angry at her and convinced the others not to come? What if it stormed and parents didn't want to venture into the country? On rare occasions like these she hated living in the country. The weather had been perfection. The turnout was fabulous! Tess was in her element. She made the rounds to make sure everyone had snacks and plenty of drinks.

She had dimmed the lights a bit lower and noticed that some of her friends had paired off into the darkest corners to steal an occasional kiss. Other more timid souls were slow dancing, most of them arm's length apart. Todd had been sitting by himself, curiously watching the dancers. She remembered plopping down beside him and asking him if he was having a good time. She had smiled at him. He had looked down at the floor and she could see him blush. He was so quiet.

Then he had looked up and looked her directly in the eyes. "Your whole face smiles when you grin, Tess. Your eyes just disappear." She was the one that had blushed. That moment that was forever etched in her heart was over in an instant.

A CHANGED REFLECTION

Tess had noticed there were a few couples dancing to the Jackson Five. She had asked Todd to dance and he promptly responded, "I don't dance." Little did she realize those three words would haunt her throughout high school. The smile she had on her face had disappeared and she had pretended to pick up a wrapper off the floor to hide her disappointment.

Then he cautiously touched her hand and told her he'd make an exception for her on the next slow song... if that was okay with her. She had felt the butterflies start to stir. She remembered feeling at a loss for something to say. THAT certainly wasn't like her. And then the most idiotic remark came out of her mouth, "Now that school's over, what are you going to do with yourself?" Who said stuff like that? Seriously.

But Todd had responded, "Probably go riding." He had started to fidget as if he wanted to say more and then suddenly he blurted out, "do you like horses? I mean, would you like to go riding sometime? Maybe tomorrow? Can I call you?"

"I would love that." He couldn't see her blush in the darkness. "I can hardly wait. But I'll warn you, it's been awhile since I've ridden," she fibbed. The thought of being that close to Todd made her quiver.

Truth be told, Tess loved riding her big beautiful chestnut quarter horse every chance she got. She spent her afternoons brushing him and telling him her secrets. He was the tall handsome gentleman in her life. She loved touching his velvet nose and feeling his hot breath on her neck. He took her wherever she wanted to go and he took her fast. Her need for speed. Their love was mutual.

"No problem," he had told her and then asked her to dance. "I like this song." That was the first time they ever danced and she remembered how warm and muscular his body felt against hers. And she remembered the song. "Colour My World." In her head it became "their song." She had chosen that song to be played at her wedding. The wedding she always believed would be to Todd. The one where she married someone else.

"I hope you'll call," Tess told him after the song had finished. How ironic. Tess would spend most of her high school days waiting by the phone, hoping Todd would call.

Todd kept that promise. He called her the very next day and rode his horse across town and into the country to get to her house. She was elated. It gave her another chance to try to figure out what it was about him that intrigued her.

She saw him ride his horse into the yard and he waited until she came outside. She thought it was just because he was shy. Looking back she now knew better. It may have started out as shyness but it turned into a control issue that only grew worse with time.

"Why don't you just ride with me on my horse," he asked her. He was riding bareback so there was no saddle to get in the way.

You just want me to snuggle up close, she thought. Okay, she was game. He helped her up, and they headed down the road. It was a warm, breezy afternoon and she could smell the aroma of fresh cut alfalfa. As the time passed she felt the warmth of the horse creating a wetness on her legs.

They started down a deserted gravel road. He turned around, and she thought maybe he had something to say to her. He was so quiet. To her surprise he kissed her tenderly for a few moments and then quickly turned back around.

She grabbed a hold of him a little tighter. She was glad he couldn't see her blush. They continued down the road in silence. *Wow*, she thought. It stirred something inside her she hadn't felt before. It was her first real kiss and it was incredible. It was the start of something she wouldn't be able to control.

The horseback riding became a weekly thing. She waited anxiously for each Saturday to arrive. Sometimes they each rode their own horse but she was always more excited when he suggested they ride together. They would find secluded spots to rest their horses.

He never said a lot but his kissing became more frequent and much more passionate. She had never known that kind of tenderness or affection. She had grown up in a family that did not show affection but she always knew she was loved. *So this is what this feels like*, she thought.

By the end of the summer they had begun exploring each other's bodies. It just seemed natural and felt amazing. With each step they took, the more she desired. It all seemed so innocent. Little did she realize how addicted she was becoming.

The school year came and went with all the trials and turmoil of junior high. She was glad when summer finally arrived.

That summer started out much like the one before. Saturdays filled with horseback riding and weekdays spent at the swimming pool. With each passing week, things progressed a little bit further. The process was so slow and gradual it didn't seem wrong. She was falling in love with Todd. Whatever love was at that early age. She only knew it was an intense feeling and she wanted it to last forever.

She remembered the day—it was a perfect summer day. There had been a light breeze, and there was not a cloud in the crystal-blue sky. The color of his eyes. She had ridden her horse to his house. "Hey, why don't you put your horse in the pasture," he said with a grin.

"Okay," she said without question. Little did she know that decision would change her life forever. He smiled that impish smile at her and grabbed her hand. She knew that look. He wanted to hold her close. How she loved his sky-blue eyes and muscular body.

"I've got to check my neighbor's house. They are on vacation. Come on." They ran across the pasture to the house. He unlocked the door and led her inside. She waited by the door while he checked the front door and alarm system.

"Come with me to check out the upstairs." He grabbed her hand and led her up the steps.

He knew every part of her body. She knew every inch of his. They had learned together. They had done everything except go all the way. They reached the top of the stairs, and he snagged the corner of her shirt and pulled it off over her head. "So this was the reason you wanted me to come over," she whispered to him with a smile. He pulled her close and kissed her. The kind of kiss that made her go weak in the knees. She loved what he did to her body. The way he made her feel. He grabbed her hand, and they headed down the hall.

They reached what appeared to be the master bedroom. Once inside the door, he grabbed her waist, and with one quick motion, he reached behind her back and had undone her bra and pulled the straps off her shoulders so that it fell to the floor. He gently cradled her breasts and buried his face into them. "You smell good," he said in a muffled voice. "Let your hair down."

She pulled away. She took the ponytail holder out of her hair and bent over and flipped her head back. Her long brown hair cascaded over her breasts and tanned shoulders. He had been watching her and smiling. He took off his shirt. He grabbed her and held her close. She loved the way skin on skin felt.

He kissed her neck. It caused her to shudder. He knew it made her hot. After a few moments, he stopped, released her, and walked over to the middle of the bedroom and lay down on the floor. "Come here, beautiful."

She had a feeling things were going past second base today. She obeyed his command and walked over and lay down beside him. He reached over her, undid her jeans and slowly slid them off, kissing every inch of her body along the way. He knew he had her under his control. Then he stood up and slipped out of his jeans.

He lay back down beside her. She slid her hands across his body. He was fully aroused. *How many more times will we be able to simply lie like this in each other's arms?* she thought as her breath became more rapid.

He straddled her and started kissing her breasts. Then he sucked on them until the nipples were hard. He started down her belly. Slowly, deliberately. She closed her eyes and concentrated on the pleasure she was feeling. He had learned what she liked.

She let out a little gasp as he moved further down and found her sweet spot. She was hot. He had figured out how to make her body convulse with pleasure. He loved watching her. She knew she had little control at this point. She was no longer thinking with her head. Their bodies were so intertwined. She pulled him close and whispered in his ear, "I want you."

"Are you sure?" he asked quietly.

She wasn't thinking of the consequences. She just knew what her body wanted. She wanted him.

They were just kids, but they had started playing grown-up games. That night as she tried to fall asleep, she couldn't stop thinking of that afternoon. A beautiful, amazing memory forever etched in her mind. She could never undo what they had done. She also knew she could no longer live without it.

"Tess," the teacher repeated, "would you please read the first chapter out loud to the class?"

Chapter Seven

———※———

She stood at the edge of the road by the guesthouse and heaved a giant sigh and smiled. "Like Groundhog Day," she mused. Repeat the day over and over again just like the movie. Leave it to Greg to make a remark like that and then get on his motorcycle and ride off.

Oh well, she thought out loud. It was probably for the best. She didn't know what she would do if he had actually pursued her. Besides, that night in her memories had happened years ago and she certainly didn't look like a twenty-year-old any longer. Sometimes memories were meant to stay simply that.

She headed back into the house. She needed some time to process. Her mind was whirling. What had just happened? The dream had been so vivid in her mind. She knew it wasn't real. But the spark he set off inside her certainly was. She hadn't had feelings like those in a very long time. Feelings that had been buried over the years.

As she started up the stairs she stopped. She walked over to the bookshelf and searched until she found her red journal. She had written in it so many years before. She wondered. She carefully turned the pages, remembering the things she had meticulously documented in her youth because it was the only way she could believe her life had made a difference. She needed to leave proof that she had existed. That there really was a girl with feelings in the reflection of the mirror that no one saw. Then, there it was. She quietly read the words out loud.

A CHANGED REFLECTION

> When you held me tonight…
> I knew things could be, yet not that they would be.
> I think you felt it too.
> Perhaps we'll never again share an evening—
> But I won't forget the precious moments,
> Of the very special one, we shared tonight.

That night. Only the most deep seeded emotions and thoughts had made it into the bound journal. Other poetry and stories were kept in notebooks or scribbled on assorted pieces of note paper. She found herself writing on all kinds of pieces of paper. It all depended on where she was when the inspiration hit. She had done it since she was ten years old. It was why she left the first time. She wanted to write. Now, she had the sudden urge again. Something was compelling her. She hadn't written in years.

Something had triggered the dream. Such vivid dreams had always signified some type of major event in her life. Her recurrent childhood dreams of flying had instilled a love of flying in her and was instrumental in her decision to skydive with her cousin Catrina. It really hadn't been a spontaneous decision. It had been hardwired in her for a very long time. She had committed to taking lessons before she jumped and had jumped ten times. The only reason she had stopped was because she had moved. She knew the dream and this encounter were trying to tell her something.

She went upstairs to change her clothes before she headed out to the dock. How she wished her mother was still alive to talk to her. She always gave her perspective on things. She was a no nonsense kind of woman. As she entered her bedroom she stopped to pick up the picture of her mother. She had never had a chance to say goodbye. "Oh mamma, what am I supposed to do?" she asked the picture quietly as the tears ran down her cheeks.

She closed her eyes and took a long and very forceful breath. "I know," she replied as she set the picture back on the dresser and wiped the tears from her cheeks. She slipped out of her clothes and grabbed a pair of sweats and a T-shirt. After pausing for a moment, she wrangled herself out of her bra as well. It was almost as if she didn't want anything to be touching her so closely.

She headed down the stairs and into the kitchen. She grabbed one of the etched sailboat glasses from the buffet. She poured Baileys into it and added ice. She pulled an old sweatshirt off the hall tree and threw it over her T-shirt. The sun was starting to set and a slight breeze had come up off the lake. She ran her fingertips through her short sassy hair. "Not those long flowing golden-brown locks anymore," she lamented out loud. But then again, she wasn't that girl anymore either.

She grabbed her glass and started to head out to the dock. She stopped and turned around and raced into the dining room and grabbed a notepad and pen from the secretary. The inspiration had returned. A writer whose writers block had been lifted after what seemed like an eternity. She loved this time of evening. No one was on the lake except for the occasional fishing boat. She reached the end of the dock and sat on the edge with her feet barely touching the water. She made little ripples with her toes. Still cold. She picked up the pen and started to write.

Then, for a moment, she closed her eyes and tried to absorb the final warmth of the sun. She needed that warmth to hug her body all over. She watched as the sun disappeared beyond the horizon. Only the faint glow in the sky remained. *One of God's greatest gifts*, she thought. Meant to be shared. She continued to write until she could no longer see the lines on the paper in the darkness.

She had been down this road before. It wasn't the first time. Lonely but not alone. Complications. Circumstances were not the same yet somehow vaguely familiar. She searched her mind. Why had she not learned from her past mistakes? The hands of the clock had been set in motion and couldn't be turned back. This much she knew. Catrina knew it too.

She let the last sip of Baileys slowly slide down her throat. She could feel a slight buzz. It didn't take much. She had learned a long time ago it was best not to drink too much. It could cloud one's judgement and start to pull the barriers down she worked so hard to keep up. Liquor was never the problem. She knew what had driven her to make some bad choices in her life. It was the same thing that compelled her to write. Loyalty and passion. Sometimes she just couldn't let go until circumstances had almost destroyed her.

It was getting cooler. The breeze was starting to pick up. It was causing the water to create small swirling patterns across the lake. She closed her eyes and listened to the water as it lapped against the boulders. She felt a sudden chill. It gave her goose bumps all over her body. She shuddered and then smiled. Goose bumps that made her think of that night.

The moment at the end of the song when he had kissed her on the nape of her neck. He had given her goose bumps and a whole lot more. And now she knew that he also remembered that night after all the years. A special night because it was forever etched in her mind and inked on paper.

She took one last huge breath of lake air into her lungs before she headed for the house. She periodically intentionally took very deep breaths. It reminded her how lucky she was just to be able to. She thought back to the time in her life when it wasn't possible and even little short breaths had caused her excruciating pain. A tear rolled down her cheek. That event had changed her forever. She would never look at things the same way again. She had the marks to constantly remind her.

The lights on the walkway had come on. She paused to look at the bank. It was such a wise investment to have the steps rebuilt and the bank reinforced with boulders. She had brought some rocks from the farm and incorporated them into the landscape. Some of the native wildflowers were starting to bloom. Her mother would have been pleased. She had loved flowers.

She still felt a chill so she knew that meant hot tub time. "Almost a perfect ending to the day," she whispered to herself and grinned. She walked around the backside of the house and headed into the spa room. She grabbed a towel from the shelf.

Even though most of the daylight was gone, getting into the spa always presented a problem since windows were on both sides of the room and neither side had blinds or shades. She glanced both ways and then slipped out of her clothes. She eased herself into the water. Hot.

She turned on the jets and lay back and let them methodically massage her lower back. It felt good. Before Greg arrived, she had worked hard and was starting to feel it in her muscles. The only thing better would have been him giving her a back massage. She closed her eyes and used her imagination. She had become very good at it. He would massage oil onto her back and then turn her over and rub oil on her front side and drive her crazy. She wondered if it really would ever be more than just thoughts in her mind.

She slid down until only her head was above the water. Almost perfect. She sighed. She knew she would have to leave the lake in the morning and return to work. That thought made her extremely sad. The lake was the only place she felt truly happy. She felt her mother's presence there. When she saw her fingertips begin to wrinkle she climbed out of the hot tub and grabbed her towel and wrapped it around her body.

If only life were simple like it was when she was at the lake. Quiet. Peaceful. No drama. She heard the barred owl call in the distance. She stood on the back step in her towel and called back, "Who cooks for you?" She waited. He answered her. She smiled. The previous summer a pair of barred owls had taken up residence in the big tree outside the lake house. She would talk to them every day, and they would watch her with their big dark soulful eyes.

She loved the birds and wildlife at the lake. She was particularly amused with the small wren that came back year after year. She had put up a little wren house in the tree by the screened porch. That wren talked all the time and often scolded her, especially if she wasn't getting her work done. She was convinced it was her mother reincarnated.

She closed the lid of the hot tub. She grabbed her silk robe from the hook by the door. She dropped her towel and slipped it on. It glided across her skin. Tess smiled. Yes, she was a very tactile person. She hadn't thought about it until Cat had pointed it out to her. Cat had a way of seeing things she often missed or chose to ignore.

A CHANGED REFLECTION

She headed into the kitchen to grab a glass of water. She opened the freezer door and added some ice and then turned and looked out at the lake. It took her breath away. It was only a half moon but it was brilliant and casting an incredible reflection in the water. It was almost as if the reflection on the water was casting a lighted path leading to the heavens. Telling her to trust in something greater than herself.

Chapter Eight

Tess knew exactly when things changed.

"Mom, I don't want to go to church camp," she pleaded with her mother. "I go to church every Sunday and I have never missed Sunday school. I know you went to that camp when you were a kid but it's not my thing." Tess didn't want to leave. The thought of a week without his touch was almost more than she could bear.

"It will be good for you," her mother replied. "It will get you away from that Cameron boy for a while." She knew her mother thought they were spending way too much time together. Tess knew deep down she was too young to be in the kind of relationship they had, but she couldn't help herself. His body and touch had become an addiction for her. The more time they spent together, the more she wanted it. "It's only for a week," her mother's voice trailed off as she headed down the stairs to do laundry.

"Fine." She knew from the tone in her mother's voice there would be no negotiating. She'd just have to make the best of it. Her friend Stacie was going and she wanted Tess to be her bunk mate. Tess decided maybe it could be a fun diversion before high school started. Several of the kids from her church were going. It was on a lake. It couldn't be all bad. What kind of trouble could it cause? It was church camp after all.

She headed upstairs and started to sort things on her bed. She looked through the list Stacie had given her and started picking out clothes that would make cute outfits. If she had to go, she was going to look good. She had always prided herself on how she looked and the fact that she had done it so wisely. She sewed a lot of her clothes and watched the sales. She made her hard earned money go a long ways. It was something she could control.

She cringed remembering the conversation she had with Todd. He didn't want her to go. He hated her being away from him. At least that was what he told her. Was it the control issue or something else? Tess had a funny feeling about the conversation but she couldn't quite put her finger on it. Something was just not right. She had fallen under his spell and her heart squelched any notions her mind might have been telling her. She had assured him it was only for a week and it was church camp after all.

That night her sleep was restless. Another sign. Restless sleep always meant there was something about to happen or that needed to happen. It had been this way with her since she had been little. Intuition. It always meant something. Sometimes it took months to present itself, but it always did.

The next morning the sun was shining brightly and the clouds were puffy and playful. The trepidation from her restless sleep was gone, at least for the time being.

Tess finished packing her suitcase and then sat down at her vanity and gently combed through her long hair one last time and then she pulled it into a ponytail. The day was already humid and she wanted the weight of her hair off her neck. If only other weights in her life could be so easily taken care of.

The girl in the mirror smiled. Little did Tess realize that genuine smile would be the last for a very long time. She grabbed her suitcase and headed downstairs. There was still time for a piece of toast and her mother's wonderful rhubarb sauce.

It was a five hour trek to the camp but the ride in the church van with her friends helped to pass the time. They arrived shortly after lunch. It truly was a beautiful place like her mother had told her. There were big old oak trees creating a wonderful shade canopy from the hot summer sun. There was a cool breeze coming off the lake and it actually felt better than the thermometer indicated.

They unloaded the van and carried their bags to the girls' cabin. Bunk assignments were given out but she didn't have to worry about it since Stacie had already put in the request for them to bunk together. Since Stacie's older sister Jackie was the camp counselor, it was a given. Tess soon found herself settling in. After dinner the girls bunk house met the boys bunk house around the campfire and s'mores. She actually found herself having a good time.

After the last piece of chocolate had been used, Jackie stood up and cleared her throat. "Tomorrow is going to be a busy day. We have auditions for the church play we will be performing for the community at the end of the week and then church ministry. In the middle of the week we will be going to the amusement park as a special treat. We don't want anyone going off on their own, so be sure you hang out in at least pairs. Make a point to get to know someone new."

"I'll be your partner Tess." She turned and realized that Mark had moved beside her at the campfire. She had met him earlier in the day. He seemed like a nice guy.

"Sure," she replied, never giving it a second thought. What could be the harm in that?

The evening ended with singing around the campfire and a prayer. "I see Mark asked to be your "pair partner" for the amusement park," her friend Stacie kidded her. She nudged her and smiled. "He's kinda cute." They headed back to their cabin.

"Yeah, whatever," Tess replied. "Jackie said to hang out in 'at least' pairs, so that means you're part of the group too."

Stacie laughed. "You got it." This was church camp. It was no big deal.

The days passed quickly and in the blink of an eye it was time to head to the amusement park. Tess threw on a pair of jean shorts and a white tank top. The white showed off the tan she had acquired during the week. They loaded onto the bus and headed to the park.

After surveying the park and checking out all the rides, Tess and Stacie decided to ride the roller coaster. After the third time, on the last curve Tess smiled and yelled so Stacie could hear her above all the screams, "We have to stop! I'm going to puke!"

"Then we have to go to the fun house!" Stacie laughed.

"Only if we can get some cotton candy first." Tess giggled. Stacie ran ahead and got in line. Tess felt a presence and turned around to see Mark following behind. "Oh, come on, you sad sack," she laughed as she grabbed his hand. Then she stopped dead in her tracks.

What was SHE doing here? thought Tess. They were hours from home. She knew Samantha had a thing for Todd. She had heard rumors. She felt a huge knot in the pit of her stomach. She knew this innocent act would be made into something other than it was to benefit Sam. Sam was the kind of girl who did whatever to get what she wanted. Tess knew Sam wanted Todd. Tess would pay the consequences.

If only she could talk to Todd first. But there were two more days of church camp. By the time she got home, the damage was done. Her friend Suzy told her that Sam had been hanging out with him and had told him "her version" of what she had seen.

Tess knew Todd was an extremely jealous and controlling person. She wasn't quite sure when it had gotten so bad. She called him as soon as she got home. She tried for two days... He wouldn't call her back. She finally got in the car and drove to his house. She stood on his front porch and rang the doorbell. He opened the door. "It's over Tess. You brought this all on yourself," he said with a look of disgust in his eyes. And with that, he turned around and slammed the door in her face.

She wanted to die on the spot. She felt her world come crashing down on her. Tears streamed down her cheeks. She got in her car and headed to the highway and drove. Fast. Tears blurred her vision. It didn't matter... maybe it would take away the pain. No one would care if she didn't come back. The blare of the horn from an oncoming car snapped her back to reality. She realized she had crossed the centerline.

She pulled off onto the shoulder and let the tears fall. Somehow through the sobs she heard the familiar voice from her dreams, "My sweet girl, it's not your time. You have so much to do." She wiped the tears from her cheeks. Grandma MEME. She often spoke to her in her dreams. It was a connection she didn't quite understand but knew she would someday have to find out.

"Oh MEME," Tess whispered. "I feel like my life is over."

Tess took the backroads home to avoid any further confrontations with traffic. She was grateful her parents were gone when she finally did get home. She parked the car in the garage and ran into the house and up the stairs to her room. How could he do this to her? Why was he believing Sam over her? She had given everything she had to him. Didn't that mean anything to him? But perhaps Sam had too. Tears streamed down her cheeks once more.

She took an album from its cover and put it on the turntable. She lay down on her bed and buried her tear stained face in her pillow. The words filled her room as she fell into a troubled sleep...

> I would give up anything I own,
> Would give up my life, my heart, my home.
> I would give everything I own,
> Just to have you back again.
> Just to touch you once again.

Chapter Nine

She snapped a picture of the tree and posted it to Facebook. It had gotten so big. It was the same tree her mother had used a few years before when she had compiled a family history. The family tree. Family was everything to Tess. She knew she would someday visit and research her great-great-grandmother MEME's birthplace.

She remembered thinking the album had so many spelling errors and was disjointed. It was not like her mother's projects. Her mother was a perfectionist.

Tess should have seen the signs. Somewhere deep down she must have known. Intuition. She had made an unexpected trip to see her mother for which she was forever grateful. She hadn't realized her mother was in a race against time. She was gone two months later. Tess missed her every day.

Perhaps that was why she felt so happy at the lake house. It was where she felt the closest to her mother. It was where she knew she needed to end up. She would eventually. It was only a matter of time.

She turned the radio on and headed down the road. She had so many miles to go before she could rest. Soon she would be in her happy place once again. The work was never ending but it didn't matter. When she started to feel overwhelmed, she took a moment and looked out over the lake. Heaven. Nothing else mattered.

She had made good time. She had driven a little faster than usual. She would have plenty of daylight to get her chores done before she would catch the beautiful sunset. She parked the car and carried her bag inside. As she returned for the groceries she noticed there was a truck circling the point. How strange. It circled twice and then parked down the road. She noticed a good-looking young man get out of the truck and start walking slowly down the road until he stopped in front of the house.

She walked down the sidewalk. "Can I help you?" He rather bashfully said yes; he needed to know where the Hennings lived. "Two doors down." He smiled and thanked her. She watched him walk away. He was wearing blue jeans and a flannel shirt. She had seen a smile like that before.

Tess knocked off her chore list as daylight evaporated quickly. Her travels had made her tired. After watching a spectacular sunset, she decided to turn in early. She grabbed her phone and headed upstairs. She stripped out of her clothes and crawled between the sheets. She snuggled in for the night.

Her phone pinged. Did she really want to even look? Curiosity got the better of her. She picked up her phone and read the message. She smiled.

"I liked your farm house. I was only inside a few times." She remembered. She had just come across a picture of him smiling and sitting in a chair in her parent's basement. There it was.

That was the smile she was remembering on the young man she had seen earlier in the day.

"Your mom was great," he continued. Her smile widened.

"Yes, she was. I miss her a lot," she responded. With that thought, she turned her phone to silent and set it back on the nightstand.

Tess missed her mother every day. She and her mother were a lot alike in some respects. Perhaps that was why they locked horns every now and again. But her mother was also her best friend. She was someone Tess knew who would always be there for her.

Now she was gone. She left so suddenly that no one had the chance to say good-bye. Tess remembered seeing her the day before she died. Something had told her she needed to go see her parents. She would be forever grateful for that sign. That morning she was leaving her mother was sitting in her chair at the kitchen desk. "I love your hair that way mom. You look so pretty."

That was the only time she had ever told her mother she looked pretty. There had been no hug good-bye, no "I love you." That wasn't the Carrington way. They weren't an overly emotional public display of affection kind of family. "Stoic" was how the doctor had described her father.

Tess knew her parents loved her deeply. They just never hugged her or told her they loved her. But she knew. The first time Tess could remember her father telling her he loved her was in the hospital room. It was a Saturday night. She had lost her baby and she knew she was sick. She remembered him looking directly into her eyes and saying he loved her. The words she replied were etched in her memory. "I love you too daddy."

It was only later she found out the doctors had told her family there was nothing they could do for her. She wasn't going to make it. A great sadness overcame her when she thought of the precious baby that didn't survive. The one she held in her arms and then said good-bye to. The one she never heard cry. "I guess they forgot to tell me, "she said quietly out loud although there was no one to hear her.

She closed her eyes tightly and once again somewhere in the distance she once again heard the words MEME had whispered so many years before to her in the car when she was stopped along the side of the road. "My sweet girl...it's not your time. You have so much to do."

Several years out of high school her mother had asked her why she had stayed with Todd for so long when he had made her so unhappy. For the first time she told her mother the truth about him. "Because he hugged me and told me he loved me." Then she had given her mother a hug and told her she loved her.

That was the day the Carrington tradition of no public display of affection started to change. A reserved change, but change none the less. Something good had finally come from something bad. When life dealt you bad cards, you had to play them to the best of your ability. She thought about the hand she was currently holding. Time would only tell how she decided to play them.

She burrowed under the covers and drifted off.

Chapter Ten

———✻———

High school had begun. Who said this was supposed to be a fun time in your life, Tess wondered? Tonight was the last football game of the season. She had to be there. She was a cheerleader. She would cheer for Todd and the team and after the game he would brush her off and tell her he had "other plans." Week after week. Why didn't she stop it? She knew. For the same reason an alcoholic can't quit drinking. Hers was an emotional addiction.

Perhaps, just perhaps, at the football game she would have an opportunity to get her "knight in shining armor" to look her direction when he came off the field. He was tall and handsome and always smiled at her in homeroom. She looked forward to homeroom. It was one place she felt safe and happy. He was there. He could take her away from her prison. His friendship meant the world to her. She knew he was the one person that could help her break the addiction.

She and Todd had gotten back together. Or as he made it clear to everyone, he "took her back." She soon found out he wasn't the lovable boy she had fallen in love with. He wasn't the same gentle and kind person she had become addicted to. The words were cruel and the tone was condescending. All of a sudden there were a new set of rules to the game they had been playing. His rules. Harsh rules. Take it or leave it. The only time she caught glimpses of the boy she fell in love with was when he was alone with her and caught up in their passion. Away from Sam.

Tess felt she had no choice. She knew it was a physical thing. He knew everything about her body and how to give her great pleasure. It had started out as an innocent game and now she was in over her head. He controlled her mind and secluded her from her friends. She had no one to talk to about it. He dominated her and she felt helpless to stop it.

Gone were her smiles and outgoing bubbly personality. She had become a quiet mousy little girl always on the verge of tears. She had become Todd's marionette. He controlled the strings. It was all about what he wanted. Ultimate control. She hardly recognized the reflection in the mirror.

The bell rang. She was the last to leave the classroom. She knew he would be at her locker waiting for her. She wondered what she had done wrong this time. It really didn't matter. It was always her fault. She was always to blame. He told her so daily.

As she already knew, he was waiting for her. His blue eyes were like ice. "If you weren't such a tramp and a liar you wouldn't be in this position," he growled at her. Her head was down so no one could see the tears welling up in her eyes. "You brought this on yourself." She wanted to die. Why couldn't she find the strength to let him go...was it because he would never totally let her go either? Perhaps deep down she fulfilled a need for him too.

She knew in her mind he was being unfaithful but it was something her heart wouldn't let her believe. She heard the talk. She had tried to confront him about it. Every time she did, he somehow turned it around and simply made her feel stupid for asking. She had given him everything. Her love, her heart, her entire being. She had believed it would be forever with him.

Now he was asking for the only thing she had left. "If you think we're going to stay together, the only way that will happen is if you quit all those damn extracurricular activities of yours. You can't be trusted in band or chorus and you're sure as hell not going to be on the yearbook staff anymore."

Tears were now rolling down her cheeks. "Stop crying. You're embarrassing me. You're such a loser sometimes. I have plans for after the game tonight so don't be hanging around waiting for me. I have to work tomorrow." He stormed off. Again, she would spend her weekend alone. She didn't dare make plans on the offside chance that after work he would call her. She had learned to wait for his call, just in case.

His words burned her soul like a cigarette butt would burn the skin. She cringed. Somehow, there had to be a way out. Tess truly believed that. Deep down she was an eternal optimist and her faith was strong. It was something her parents had instilled in her. This could not be what God had planned for her.

She somehow made it through her chemistry lab and economics class. She talked to no one. She just did her work and remained quiet. An overwhelming sense of sadness engulfed her. Her mother's voice popped into her head, "Suck it up." She was so thankful that it was Friday.

After the last bell rang she quickly left the school. She was so glad her parents let her drive herself to school on Fridays. It was her reward for good grades. She didn't want anyone asking her what the latest drama was about on the bus, and there was no way she was waiting around school to ride home with her mother. She was tired of making up excuses and living the lies.

She was glad her dad was out working in the field when she got home. She only wanted him to be proud of her. She couldn't let him know how she had failed him.

She grabbed an apple from the refrigerator and went up to her room. She got out her journal. She found great solace in her writing. It was her escape. Her connection to a life that had meaning. She knew she had talent. It had been confirmed by the certificate and letter she had received from the National Poetry Press. She took the letter from the back of her journal and read the words slowly.

"In view of the great number of entries from your state, we congratulate you on your achievement. May we suggest that in view of this accomplishment, you should continue with your writing and keep working at it whenever you can." She knew she was meant to write, to document her feelings. She needed to tell a story. Words could create a world that she could thrive in. She could somehow make things better through her words. Perhaps someday she would be able to look back and understand the feelings. Someday she would write a story and share it.

A CHANGED REFLECTION

Music was her other great escape whether it was listening to it or playing it. When she was home alone she would sit at the piano and play. She was not very good but she knew if she really practiced and gave it much effort she could be. She smiled as she noticed the clarinet case in the corner of the room. Something she had given up … to feed her addiction. She had learned to play *Stranger on the Shore* for her father. It was his favorite. Someday she would play it again.

Her music and her writing were the only things that kept her grounded. Sometimes they were the only things that gave her enough reason to continue. That and the reoccurring words from MEME that came in her sleep. She sat on the floor by her albums and shuffled through them. She settled on Pure Prairie League and placed it on the turntable and turned the knob. The album dropped on the spindle. She closed her eyes and listened as music filled her room and she drifted away…

> Falling in and out of love with you
> Falling in and out of love with you
> Don't know what I'm gonna do
> I keep falling in and out of love…

"Tess, you're going to be late for the last game of the season," her mother yelled from the bottom of the stairway. Her voice snapped her back to reality.

"Okay Mom." Tess got up and quickly sat down at her vanity and touched up her makeup, put a smile on her face and headed downstairs. She would "suck it up" the way her mother taught her. She had become an expert at putting on a "happy" façade even though her heart ached.

It was the last game of the season. That thought made her sad. It meant the end of cheerleading for the year. She loved being a cheerleader. It made her feel special. She actually loved football and the thrill of the guys winning and the excitement of the crowd truly made her happy. Winter sports were not an option. He made sure of that.

Didn't he understand that she loved him with all her heart and entire being? The heart wants what the heart wants. If he couldn't love her like that then deep down she knew it wasn't the right thing.

Maybe that was why she subconsciously was searching for her Prince Charming. Perhaps that was why when Greg smiled at her in homeroom she knew there was something there that could be. "Oh, MEME, what am I to do? I'm not strong like you," she whispered. She headed down the stairs.

"Bye Mom. I'll be home after the game. Don't wait up." She smiled.

"Just behave yourself," her mother called after her as she headed out the door. She hopped into the car and backed it out of the garage. Before she could turn the radio on another thought crossed her mind. "Okay, admit it, Tess," she said to herself. "You secretly hope Greg will finally notice you and miraculously ask you out."

She looked into the rear view mirror at her reflection and smiled. You couldn't blame a girl for dreaming.

Chapter Eleven

Tess looked out the bedroom window toward the lake. It was going to be another beautiful day. There were only slight ripples on the water. Time to get the boat cleaned up and ready for the season. It wasn't her favorite job but she knew once it was done it would be another means in which to escape. The boat wasn't big but it had a large inboard engine that could streak across the lake with ease on a calm day. This day.

She threw on a pair of shorts over her swimsuit before heading downstairs. *Might as well get some rays*, she thought. No need to be lacking in vitamin D! Tess loved the way the sun made her feel. It warmed her body and soul. It helped her feel happiness. Happiness she had been searching for. A happiness that she longed for but something that continued to elude her.

Tess searched through the utility closet but didn't spot the rags she was looking for. She headed to the basement and grabbed some from the shelf by the dryer. She headed back upstairs and grabbed a bottle of suntan lotion from the bathroom. She found herself humming. Or perhaps it was more like a kitten purring. Like Buttercream. Wow. She hadn't thought about that kitty for a very long time. The thought of the long haired yellow and white kitten scampering through the grass to come see her made her smile.

Her intuition told her it was going to be a very good day. Perhaps she should be whistling. Wasn't it whistle while you work? Whistling. That meant it was teatime. Once she found the bucket in the spa room she threw her rags inside. She returned to the kitchen and put the teakettle on. While she waited for it to blow off steam she gathered the cleaning supplies from the utility closet. Once that was accomplished she rummaged through the refrigerator until she found the last bran muffin.

On a whim she had decided to make bran muffins the weekend before. Her mother had always made them. She was missing her mother and found it a way to connect with her. She made them the way her mother always had—with a surprise inside. She stuck the muffin in the microwave and warmed it for a few seconds. It would be perfect with her morning tea.

Soon the teakettle was spouting off. "Yes, I hear you. I know you're hot, and I am coming. Just be patient, Mr. Kettle. You get worked up so easily." She chuckled to herself on the little play on words. Tess loved words and loved to tease. She always had and that trait had gotten her in trouble more than once but it was something she just couldn't change. It was part of her mischievous nature. Something she had inherited from her father.

She grabbed her cup of tea and muffin and settled in her chair at the dining room table. Her mother's chair that had now become her assigned seat. She smiled as she remembered her mother sitting there talking about something but always talking. Now that was a trait she had inherited from her mother!

Tess slowly split her muffin in two. The warmed strawberry jam oozed out. The surprise! She had always loved it as a child and her inner child still delighted in it. Perhaps that was why she loved Christmas so much. Not for presents for herself but to see the surprise and delight as others opened gifts. It filled her with such happiness.

She drifted to thoughts of happy times gone by as she slowly ate her muffin and sipped on her tea. She wondered if she would ever find that kind of happiness again. Tess sighed. No she wouldn't—but a smile slowly formed on her face as her mind continued to run away with itself. She would find and create a new kind of happiness. It might take some time but she knew she wouldn't settle for anything else.

She put her dishes in the sink and grabbed a bottle of water from the refrigerator and went back to the dining room and sat down to put on her water shoes. She might have to get in the water to clean the outside of the boat and she certainly didn't want to cut herself on the razor sharp mussel shells that had invaded the lake.

She knew if she worked hard and fast she would have more time to spend out on the water. "You have to pay if you want to play," her father's voice echoed in her head. She smiled. Her mother was the rock and had taught her how to be strong. Her father taught her that if you worked hard for a while, you still had plenty of time for play. And play was important. She scooped up her phone from the porch and headed to the dock.

Distractions. Her daughter had repeatedly told her she was ADHD. Maybe. She just had so many things to do that sometimes it took her awhile to do them because on her way to one task she often saw another. When something was starring her in the face it was hard to ignore and she needed to deal with it. She stopped and sighed. She knew that applied to her work ethic. Why couldn't it apply to all aspects of her life?

She set the bucket down on the steps to the landing and tended to her flowers. Her mother loved flowers. Perhaps that was an inherited gene. Tess just knew that when she saw beautiful flowers, she thought of her mother. She felt her mother's presence at the lake house. Perhaps that was one reason she planted so many flowers there. She carefully plucked away the dead stems. Within minutes the pots of flowering plants looked lovely again. A gentle breeze crossed her face. A kiss from her mother.

She picked up the bucket and headed down to the end of the dock. She tossed the bucket into the front of the boat and then carefully climbed into the boat. One wrong move on the dewy dock, and she might find herself doing the splits for no apparent reason. She had done that before, and it wasn't a pretty picture. Once she was settled inside she grabbed her phone and found the Pandora app and put on some tunes and got busy. She started at the bow and then she would work her way back. It was a process. *Everything is a process. It just takes time*, she thought to herself.

Tess got lost in her work but knew she had made progress. The end was near. She was sprawled out across the back of the boat trying to get the last bit of dirt. She found herself singing along with

Luke Bryan, *"I don't want this night to end..."* Luke was so right. She sighed and smiled. She hadn't wanted that night to end either. The night from years gone by that was haunting her dreams. She wanted to experience it again. Like Groundhog Day.

"What night was that?" she heard a familiar deep voice say. That wasn't part of the song. She pulled the earbuds out of her ears.

"What the..." She turned around, and her whole face smiled. "What are you doing here?" she asked curiously.

"You're always telling me how good the fishing is here. So we should go fishing," he said as he winked at her. "I'll grab my pole and you can relax and catch some rays. I've got a picnic packed in my cooler," he said with a grin. "You told me I owed you lunch. You had texted me what was on your agenda today, so I took a chance you would be here. Nothing ventured, nothing gained."

She laughed.

"What's so funny?" he asked her.

I'll grab your pole all right, she thought. "Nothing, I just had an amusing thought cross my mind. For me to know and you to find out," she said with a twinkle in her eyes. His smile made her happy. The kind of happiness she had been searching for. This was turning out to be a really good day.

Greg darted off the dock and returned moments later with his fishing pole, tackle box and cooler. He climbed into the boat. Once inside she started the motor and turned on the water pump. She leaned over the side to make sure the excess water was draining.

"Nice ass," he said with a chuckle.

Tess had drained the water from the boat a hundred times. It was such a habit she hadn't thought what the view would be from his vantage point. She felt herself blush. Once the water stopped she flipped the switch.

She looked over at him as she untied the boat and pushed it away from the dock. He was not quite settled. *Fair play*, she thought and she thrust the throttle forward. The jolt caught him off guard and he quickly grabbled the windshield to regain his balance. She wrinkled up her nose and smiled at him.

"You never change, Tess," he laughed. "Guess that's what I like about you."

The lake was smooth so the boat glided across the water. She knew the perfect spot and since it was early in the year it wouldn't be packed with the crazies. She slowed the boat down, and Greg finally felt it was safe to relax a bit. "You like to go fast, don't you?" He grinned at her.

"Not in everything." She smiled back at him. "Will this spot work for you?"

"As long as the fish are biting here," he replied.

Oh, something will be biting, but it may not be the fish, she thought to herself.

"Tess, you've got that strange grin on your face again. What's going on in that pretty little head of yours?"

The thoughts in her head made her giggle out loud. He looked at her with a smile.

"Do tell."

She just shook head with a sly smile.

She dropped the anchor and then spread a towel across the backseat. Then she methodically lay back on the seat and adjusted herself, teasing him. She knew he was watching her from the corner of his eyes. "Are you comfy?" he finally asked her.

"Very," she remarked with a grin. She closed her eyes. She felt the sun warm her skin and the gentle breeze blow through her hair. The waves were gently rocking the boat. She heard his line plunk into the water.

She pulled the straps of her suit off her shoulders so she could avoid tan lines. "Better put some lotion on, or you'll get a bad burn," he told her. She threw him the bottle.

"Be a dear and take care of that for me please," she said impishly.

"Glad to help out," he said with that grin she remembered from homeroom. He had aged gracefully. His hair was shorter and peppered with gray. His tanned face had signs of getting older. His eyes were still brilliant blue. She sighed. No longer a cute boy but very much a handsome man.

He put some lotion on his hands and started to rub it into her neck. "Wow, you have some major kinks in your neck. I better work on these." He put his fingers on her shoulders and started applying a gentle pressure with his thumbs.

"Oh my," she cooed. "That feels sooo amazing." She was melting under his touch. "Don't stop." She closed her eyes and concentrated on his touch.

"I hadn't planned to." He smiled. "I like to finish the things I start." She opened her eyes and tilted her head back. She looked him directly in his eyes.

"And just exactly what have you started?" she questioned him. She really needed to know what was going on in his head. She knew what he had started for her. It was a dangerous road. She had been down that road before. She knew herself, and she knew she couldn't turn back now.

"Well"—he grinned at her—"to use the words of a cute little brunette I know, for me to know and you to find out."

A challenge. She had never backed down from a challenge in her life. She was not about to start now.

Chapter Twelve

---※---

Tess was finally able to sit in her chair by the lake with a drink and rest. She looked at the clock. Eight p.m. She had been going for over twelve hours. She knew this was what her life was going to become in order to keep the house. It didn't matter. She loved it at the lake. Watching the sunset made her realize nothing else mattered. It was beautiful.

She took a deep breath in and smelled a campfire. She loved campfires. The way the flames danced entranced her. The crackle and popping of the wood made her smile.

In the distance she heard the rapid fire of a woodpecker working hard. His drilling sounded like a toy machine gun. She realized when she listened carefully she heard many different birds. Sounds that too often went unnoticed. The sun was setting. It wasn't as stunning as the night before. Clouds were coming in. She suddenly felt a cool breeze. The wind had changed directions. Something was brewing.

She remembered she hadn't watered the flowers. The broom was still out and she needed to finish sweeping the remainder of the sidewalk she had left undone earlier in the day. She heard her barred owls in the distance. She loved their sound. One summer two of them had lived in the big tree in her yard. She talked to them every day, and they watched her with their large pensive dark eyes.

Tess set down her drink, went to the back, grabbed her broom, and quickly finished sweeping. When she had reached the street, she looked up. The neighbors across the way were outside enjoying a campfire. That was where the wonderful smell was coming from.

She knew she should walk the circle but she figured she had gotten enough exercise in for the day. Her mother was smiling down on her. There were no nagging voices in her head. Tess returned to her special spot by the lake. The darkness had crept in. She decided to totally focus on the wonder of the night.

The moon was creating a river of a thousand diamonds sparkling on the lake. It was mesmerizing. She loved the way the moonlight danced on the water. The sounds of the water lapping up against the rocks were lulling her into a sense of peace. It was a much needed feeling. The warm summer night air gently caressed her face.

Tess sat quietly in her little alcove by the lake and took in the beauty of the lake. She looked in the distance and could see bursts of color exploding over the tops of the trees. Fireworks. She could hear the faint *boom, boom, boom*.

She closed her eyes and let her soul relax and just listened. The lapping of the waves soothed her. Then there it was again. Boom, boom, boom. There was something oddly familiar about it. It was triggering something in her mind, she just couldn't quite place it. She continued to listen to the waves gently splashing along the rocks. And then it dawned on her.

It was the song. She had heard that song dozens of times. She had listened to it when she was weight training but she really only knew the refrain. She picked up her phone and searched YouTube until she found the song. What was the rest of it? She closed her eyes and started to listen...

> Do you ever feel like a plastic bag,
> Drifting through the wind, wanting to start again?

How appropriate. There was nothing she wanted more at that moment than to try to start again. She had lost herself and desperately needed to find out who she really was. She knew that the person that could change her life was no longer the girl in the reflection in the mirror. She could feel teardrops in the corner of her eyes. A sadness slowly creeped over her. She continued to listen.

A CHANGED REFLECTION

> Do you ever feel, feel so paper thin
> Like a house of cards, one blow from caving in?

Fragile. She hated the way it felt. There were days that she would find herself so completely engulfed in sadness. She would have to remind herself that sometimes the best thing to do is not think, not wonder, not imagine, not obsess. Just breathe, and have faith that everything would work out for the best.

Faith was something she had never lost along the way. Her parents had instilled a strong faith in her at a very early age. She touched the palms of her hands together and gently folded her fingers down. She rested her chin on her fingers.

> Do you know that there's still a chance for you
> 'Cause there's a spark in you?

Tess sighed. With her fingers still entwined she said a little prayer asking for help in finding her way. Was there really a spark left in her?

She had just gotten back from a conference she had gone to with Kate. During the break times they had gotten into some deep discussions. Kate was completely shocked by what Tess had told her. Tess had never before told a living soul. She wasn't even sure why she had told Kate. Perhaps it was because she desperately needed to tell someone. It was the same type of shame she had felt as a teenager. Humiliation.

"But you're so vibrant, it's just not right!" Kate had said in utter disbelief. Tess knew that better than anyone. It had been her dark unhappy secret. But telling someone had somehow released something inside her. Something was changing.

> You just gotta ignite the light and let it shine
> Just own the night like the Fourth of July
> 'Cause, baby, you're a firework
> Come on, show 'em what you're worth
> Make 'em go, "Aah, aah, aah"
> As you shoot across the sky-y-y

She thought back to the night when Greg had first texted her. Something had been ignited. The chemistry she had felt for him years before had not diminished. It was still there and she couldn't quite describe it. She had tucked that feeling away a long time ago but it had found her again. The door to her passions had been unlocked and she had stepped across the threshold and she couldn't go back. She didn't want to go back. She wanted to be the firework.

> You don't have to feel like a wasted space
> You're original, cannot be replaced
> If you only knew what the future holds
> After a hurricane comes a rainbow

Tess didn't know what the future held. She did know the significance a rainbow held in her life. The promise, having faith. She just knew she couldn't settle anymore. She had always settled. She had missed an opportunity those many years before. She didn't want to continue to exist without passion in her life. It was the one thing that she was constantly searching for. She was too young to let it all go.

> Maybe a reason why all the doors are closed
> So you could open one that leads you to the perfect road
> Like a lightning bolt, your heart will glow
> And when it's time you'll know

Greg had handed her the key. She had unlocked the door and opened it. Now she had to follow the road in front of her. She knew it wouldn't be easy. He had asked her why she had never told him the way she felt. She told him she didn't know. But she did know. She heard the fireworks booming in the distance across the lake again. The moon lit up the night sky and the fireworks reflection danced on the water.

> Boom, boom, boom
> Even brighter than the moon, moon, moon
> It's always been inside of you, you, you
> And now it's time to let it through-ough-ough

A CHANGED REFLECTION

A transformation had started. Ignite the light. She knew somewhere in her being there was a girl who needed to find her way home. Her phone pinged. She looked at her phone and smiled.

It was her friend Carolyn who had challenged her after her mother had died. It was at another conference and Carolyn had asked Tess if she could use her as her guinea pig for the life game they were role playing. Carolyn had gotten so into her face that she had made Tess cry. A good cry. The whole group had cried for her too. They could hear the intentions in her voice.

That night at dinner Tess was lucky enough to be assigned to Carolyn's table and they had a deep discussion about the future. She remembered Carolyn telling her she needed to let her intentions be known. People could not know what they didn't know. The following week she had had the discussion with her father about the lake house. She had let her intentions be known. It was the start of the process that had made the lake house a reality for her.

Tess slowly read the message Carolyn had sent her. "No matter how long we have traveled the wrong road, we can always turn around." She was telling Tess something.

Another sign.

Chapter Thirteen

---※---

"Tess?"

She had been deep in thought. She knew that voice. Her heart skipped a beat. She could hear the fireworks in the distance. She suddenly felt goose bumps everywhere. She turned around slowly. She looked up the steps and smiled.

"You look beautiful in the moonlight. I can even see that twinkle in your eyes." She couldn't move. He came down the steps slowly and stood by the chair. "More music?" He smiled. His smile. What was it about his smile that turned her inside out? "What are you listening to now?"

"Katy Perry," she said in a whisper.

He grinned and looked across the lake and saw the fireworks in the distance. "Hmmmm. You ARE a firework," he said, guessing. "And you do make me go ahh, ahh, ahh," he said, laughing as he sat down beside her.

He had gotten inside her head. He knew more about her than anyone in her life. He understood her. He knew her past and he knew the things that drove her wild. He accepted her for who she was. He was the only guy she had never lied to. Why did things have to be so complicated?

She realized the night air was sending a chill through her body and her sundress was giving away her secrets and he was watching her. "Come here. You're cold," he said as he gently grabbed her hand and pulled her onto his lap and held her tight. He rubbed up and down her back to try to warm her. As she felt his hand get lower on her back she knew he would find out her secret.

A CHANGED REFLECTION

"Well, no wonder you're cold. You don't have a stitch on under that little sundress of yours." He grabbed her chin so he could look directly into her eyes. "You naughty girl," he laughed. "Come on, it's a perfect night for a drive. I've got a sweatshirt in the truck you can put on." He gently kissed her forehead and lifted her off his lap and stood up beside her.

She turned and headed up the steps. He goosed her on the last step. She let out a little squeal. Déjà vu. She ran ahead. It didn't take him long to catch up to her and grab her hand. He had big, warm wonderfully strong hands. "Holy crap, your hands are cold!" he said in a startled voice. He tightened his grip trying to warm them.

"Cold hands, warm heart." She smiled.

"You know that smile drives me crazy," he sighed. She giggled. They had reached his truck, and he grabbed his sweatshirt and handed it to her. "Put this on you, crazy girl. I don't want you getting sick."

"Whatever you say. Since you're driving you can be the boss." Secretly she wanted him to take control and be the boss. She slipped the worn sweatshirt over her head. "Nice fit don't you think," she snickered as she twirled around for him to see. It covered up her sundress totally.

"If I didn't know better I'd think you didn't have a stitch on under that." He grinned. He helped her up in the truck. His hand slid up under the sweatshirt and dress. "I guess you really don't have much on. Sorry, my hand slipped," he said with a big grin on his face.

"I'm sure it did...on purpose, "she said winking at him. He closed the door behind her. She grabbed the sweatshirt and pulled it over her nose and took a deep breath. She loved the way it smelled. His smell. She tried to burn the memory into her head.

He hopped in the driver's side and put the truck in gear. "Hey...it's kinda lonely over here. Do I have to find a sharp curve in the road so I can make an SOB turn?"

"Slide over baby? Only if you promise to behave," she said with a smile. She hadn't heard that slang in ages. She slid over and snuggled close to him. He was warm and it felt good. Being that close to him made her feel safe.

"So where are we going?" Tess asked. She looked at him. He was studying her face. She could usually hold her own with guys, but he was different. She was nervous around him. He triggered a spark in her. He always had and after all these years he still did. She couldn't explain it but he made her feel things very few guys ever had. And there was that night.

"Well, it's a beautiful night for a drive. You're a beautiful woman. There are fireworks across the lake and I know a great spot to watch them. It's quiet and away from the crowds." He kissed her softly on the top of her head and put one arm around her and the other on the wheel.

"Sounds good to me." It was exactly what she wanted with him. Alone time and moonlight. The perfect combination. Moonlight was kinder to a person than bright sunshine. It hid the years and the imperfections better.

He pulled her a little closer and they drove in silence. She could feel the butterflies churning in her stomach. She grabbed his hand and held it to her cheek. So warm and strong. She knew he could do amazing things with those hands. She remembered.

The truck slowed and he turned down a small country lane. *A country boy at heart*, she thought. *They know all those special little back roads.* He pulled the truck off the road and into a clearing. "I've got a blanket in back."

"How convenient." She smiled. It was as if he could read her mind. Fireworks were always best laying down and staring up into the big night sky.

They walked until they found a fairly level grassy spot. He laid the blanket down for her. "After you," he said, grinning. God, how she loved his smile.

She sat down and settled in on the blanket. He watched her curiously. "Aren't you going to join me? I'm lonesome down here all by myself," she said in a little girl voice.

He laughed. "If you think for one minute I'm going to let you be a lonesome helpless little girl, you've got another thing coming." He sat down beside her. She closed her eyes and took a deep breath.

She felt so relaxed and safe with him. She lay back and opened her eyes and smiled at him.

"Look up into the sky behind the fireworks. The stars are brilliant against the dark backdrop. You don't see that in the city," he commented. Tess sighed. There were a lot of things she didn't like about the city and her life.

"Snuggle with me. Just hold me close." She closed her eyes again as she felt herself totally relaxing.

"Well, only after I…" She opened her eyes abruptly. She had a cautious look in her eyes as she glanced his direction.

"After you what?" she dared him.

"Tickle you," he said as he grabbed her and laughed.

"No fair," she giggled. "You know how ticklish I am and will give in to just about anything not to be tickled."

"I hadn't forgotten." He smiled impishly. He was tickling her sides but she felt his hands moving underneath the sweatshirt. Warm strong hands. His touch was no longer that of tickling but more of a passionate caress. He was looking directly into her eyes. "Take the sweatshirt off."

She sat up and slowly removed the sweatshirt. She knew he was all about the visual so she might as well give him a little show. He continued to stare directly into her eyes as she obeyed him. "Now the dress."

"You're a bad boy," she said as she stood up and slowly slipped the straps off her shoulders and the dress fell to the ground.

"Still beautiful," he sighed. He grabbed her hand and pulled her back down onto the blanket next to him.

"You're going to have to keep me warm," she whispered into his ear.

"Oh, I will," he promised. "But tell me, what is it you always say you like so much?" She straddled him and carefully undid the buttons on his shirt.

"Skin on skin." She pulled his shirt open and snuggled into his warm body. "Skin on skin," she whispered again into his ear and let her tongue slide across his earlobe.

He rolled her onto her back, stood up, and quickly took off his jeans. She smiled at him as if she had created a masterpiece. It was obvious she had aroused him. "You always said I was a tease in school... well, we're not in school anymore, so I promise I won't tease you."

He grinned and lay down beside her. "Now it's my turn to tease you," he laughed. He gently kissed her lips and then kissed her neck. She started to coo. "Oh my dear, this is just the beginning." He continued to kiss her and started drawing little circles on her belly with his tongue as he caressed her breasts with his hands. She started to squirm.

She felt herself let out a little gasp. His tongue was no longer on her belly but inside her. She tried to close her legs, but he grasped both legs with his hands and wouldn't let her. "Not this time," he whispered to her. It was now his finger inside her and his tongue dancing on her clit. She was losing control. Her body started convulsing.

"I need you," she begged.

"Not just yet. I like seeing you lose yourself. I'm enjoying this vision and want to savor it awhile longer. Let yourself really go, Tess," he said softly as he slowly moved his body up against hers and continued the caresses with his fingers. She tried to grab his hand but he intercepted it and held it tight. "Feel it." Her body went rigid again.

He paused long enough to let her catch her breath and then he grabbed her other hand and held them above her head and slid on top of her. She wrapped her legs around him as he thrust himself into her. "Don't stop until I feel your warmth inside of me," she begged him.

"I won't, Tess," he whispered in her ear. How could she ever explain how wonderful he felt inside her? She didn't want the feeling to end.

"Tess," he whispered in her ear and nudged her gently. "The fireworks are over and I better take you home. You fell asleep. But you must have been having a helluva dream!"

"Trust me, I was," she replied and smiled at him. The fireworks were far from over.

Chapter Fourteen

"I'm sorry. It's not happening. I'm done with your lies," Tess told him. Somewhere deep in her soul she was finding the strength to stand up for herself. She saw a determined young woman in the reflection of his eyes. A reflection she hadn't seen before. Her instincts were gnawing at her like an animal trying to free itself from a trap. Her mind was telling her to be strong, to believe in herself. Her heart was faltering.

"Todd, I SAW you. You can't talk your way out of it this time. I'm not that stupid." Tess closed her eyes and willed herself to stay strong. When she opened her eyes and looked up she could see her Spanish teacher silently cheering her on from behind him. She tried hard not to smile. It would only hurt him more and that was not her intent. *Wow*, she thought to herself. *Even my teachers are cheering for me. Even they are proud of me for finally standing up for myself.*

Todd softly touched her arm and continued pleading with her but she wasn't really listening. She had to shut him out. His touch stirred feelings inside her. "Stop," she told herself. He hadn't changed. He had tried this song and dance with her before and she always ended up getting hurt. She had to go cold turkey. She wasn't sure she could.

Her senior year. Her birthday was only a month away, and she was telling HIM it was over. It felt good. She had Jim Tanner to thank for that. Jim's sister Sandy was one of her few close friends in school. Todd had allowed that relationship to happen because Sandy dated his cousin Al. Sandy had an older brother Jim that flirted with

Tess when they were at Sandy's house. Tess realized she really enjoyed the attention and the butterflies he created.

There was some type of chemistry between them. She wasn't exactly sure what. She did know he treated her like a lady. He opened car doors for her and was proud to be with her in front of his friends. And he told her how pretty she was. Whatever it was, she liked it and wanted it to continue.

Todd had gone to Texas with his family for Christmas break. Jim had asked her to a Christmas party. She was excited to go. She needed some happiness without all the drama and hurt. She had had a great time and was delighted to find out he was a wonderful kisser when they ended up under the mistletoe. They went out several times during Christmas break. They had fun and he made her feel special.

When Todd got back and found out what had happened, he was furious even though they were broken up. His anger didn't matter to Tess this time. She wasn't afraid of it. Someone else had finally asked her out and made her feel good about herself. Jim made her realize she really did have something to offer. He was older and wasn't afraid of Todd. Todd didn't intimidate Jim. She had finally met someone who was willing to have a relationship with her that couldn't be bullied away. It made her start to realize that perhaps she wasn't really the person Todd brainwashed her into believing. The control was slowly slipping away.

"Tess, please." Maybe he really did love her. She was conflicted. Jim was making her happy and treated her like someone special. It seemed like forever since Todd had treated her that way. Tess knew the physical connection to Todd was intense, an addiction. No, not this time. "Stop," she told herself. She deserved better than that. "I'm really sorry, Todd. It's over."

For the first time, it was Todd who walked away sad. The bell rang and she headed to class. Something told her it wasn't going to end there. It wasn't going to be as easy as that. But for now she was going to enjoy her moment of freedom. The little girl that was so in love with life was starting to make a comeback.

Maybe, she thought, *others will notice me too*. Maybe HE would notice. She knew he had a girlfriend. He always had a girlfriend, but then, why wouldn't he? He was cute and clever and had a smile that made all the girls weak in the knees. Why couldn't she ever be that girlfriend? At least she could flirt with him now and not be punished for it. In the meantime, she would have fun with Jim. She knew he wasn't her forever person, but they definitely could have a good time together for the moment.

She had picked out a nice tight fitting hot pink sweater with a scoop neck to wear to school that day. She was finally feeling happy and wanted people to notice her. She wanted HIM to notice. She headed down the hall to class. Her next class just happened to be down the hall where his locker was and she was in luck. He was talking with a couple of his buddies. "Hi guys. Good luck with the basketball game tonight." She gave them her best little flirtatious grin she had.

Greg stopped and took notice. "Thanks, Tess," he said with a smile. *That wonderful smile*, she thought. It always made her heart skip a beat. Would she ever be able to show him just how much? "I can't figure that girl out," he said to his friend Kevin. "But I'd sure like to try."

Mission accomplished Tess thought as she walked away and a grin widened across her face. It felt good to be so happy. She had to savor the moments because she didn't know how long they would last. For now she would enjoy her new freedom at school and let the cards fall where they may with Jim. She knew he really wasn't her type but it didn't matter. *What the heck*, she thought. He's a good kisser and for now that was good enough. It will fill her need for touch.

Tess had decided to hang out with some girls before the basketball game. She couldn't remember the last time she had actually been invited to. The New Year was turning out better than she had hoped. The group decided to grab something to eat at the A&W before the basketball game started. Jim was busy with work so there were no conflicts. Everyone was happy, with the exception of Todd.

After the group ate, they scooped the loop before the basketball game started. Tess was excited to see Greg play. She was going out with Jim, but secretly it was Greg she hoped would give her a second look. She didn't know what it was about him but he set off a spark in her. He had ever since junior high. She loved his voice and the way his eyes sparkled when he smiled. She was such a sucker for a guy with a great smile. A genuine smile.

She was sad when the game ended and he had taken off with a group of guys. *Story of my life,* she thought. She headed to her car. She noticed a package on the front seat. She could tell from the handwriting it was from Todd. She opened the sack and saw a cassette. She turned the car on and popped it in the cassette player and started to listen.

"Really?" she said out loud to herself as she shook her head. Neil Sedaka was singing away...

> Don't take your love away from me
> Don't you leave my heart in misery
> If you go then I'll be blue
> 'Cause breaking up is hard to do.
> Remember when you held me tight
> And you kissed me all through the night
> Think of all that we've been through
> Breaking up is hard to do.

Tess stared at the dashboard as if the cassette player was going to talk to her. He had to be kidding. What part of no did he not understand? In the past he had always been able to get her to come back at the drop of a hat. Things were different this time. She was different.

The tables were turned and this time he didn't want to let her go. Somewhere in the back of her mind she wondered whether she could really let him go. Or maybe it was just what she needed from him that she couldn't let go of.

Chapter Fifteen

---※---

Tess slowly sipped the Baileys she had poured over ice. She grabbed her knees and curled up in her favorite chair by the lake in anticipation of watching another beautiful sunset. The last remnants of warmth from the sun caressed her face. Her mother's touch. She closed her eyes and concentrated on the tiny bit of heat that was left in the day. She tried to absorb it into her soul.

It was good she didn't mind being alone. She had spent much of her life that way. It was amazing how lonely one could be even when they were not alone. She had not been alone but she had been very lonely for a long time. She knew it was something she could no longer accept in her life.

She heard her phone ping. She glanced at it long enough to see it was a cartoon from her coworker. She smiled. She always seemed to know when she needed a little lift. She picked up her phone and clicked on the message to read it. "Don't feel bad laundry … nobody's doing me either." She let out a huge sigh. If it weren't really true it might actually be funny.

How ironic that one of the main reasons she had stayed in a hurtful relationship in high school was her need for passion and physical contact. Now she was in a relationship where there was no physical hurt but there was also no passion or physical contact. She knew he loved her in his own way but their lives had drifted apart. Worlds apart. It hadn't been weeks or months. It had been years. It was as if a part of her had died. She hadn't even realized the extent of her unhappiness until Greg had happened back into her life and had created a spark in her. No matter where this reconnected relationship took her, she owed him more than she could ever repay. She took another sip. A tear rolled down her cheek.

Her phone pinged again. *Let's hope this cartoon is funnier than the last*, she thought to herself. She picked up the phone. Her sadness was instantly replaced with a huge smile. She recognized the number immediately.

"Are you at the lake?" the text read.

"Yes," she texted back. "Just me and my Baileys."

"Thought it would be a perfect night for a campfire at the farm. I'm on my way there and you said you wanted to see it. I thought you might be interested." She could feel the butterflies churn in her stomach. "I can be there in ten minutes if you're game. Let me know."

No sooner had he finished texting when she texted him back, "Count me in!"

She grabbed her glass and ran up the steps and into the house. She had hoped someday he would show her his family farm. It seemed to be a common bond they shared. Generations of farmers... tilling the soil. Something you can't explain to someone. You just understood and knew. She understood and he knew it.

She changed into her hot pink panties and bra and slipped into her new jeans. No name, she never had been into the name brands. As long as they made her look and feel good, who cared? She turned her head and looked at her backside in the mirror. "Not bad." She smiled to herself.

Now for a cute little shirt. She decided on a semi-sheer white scoop neck that showed off all her curves and her new hot pink lacey bra. "Might as well give him something nice to look at." She grinned and laughed. She loved playing the game.

She took a brush to her hair and put on some hot pink lip gloss to match her bra. She grabbed the perfume bottle and sprayed a fine mist gently over her body. Not too much. Just enough to create a memory.

She heard the purr of a motorcycle circle the point. *Sweet*, she thought. He had promised her a ride on his bike. It was the perfect evening for a ride. The night was warm, but the air was cool enough to make you want to hold on tight to share body warmth.

A CHANGED REFLECTION

That thought made her smile. She bounded down the stairs. It was nice to feel so happy.

She opened the door just as he pulled in the drive. He parked his bike and took off his helmet. "Hey, there. Did you put on those tight jeans for me?" He smiled.

"You know it," she laughed as she flitted around in a little circle for him. "It's like the Katy Perry song... *I'm gonna get your heart racing in my skin tight jeans... be your teenage dream tonight.*"

She gave him a big hug. Her heart skipped a beat. He made her feel so alive. Almost like a teenager again. Once their embrace ended, he held her at arm's length and looked into her eyes. "You do get my heart racing, Tess." She felt herself blushing. He grinned. How his smile drove her crazy.

"Hop on. Here's a helmet." She took the helmet from him and strapped it on. She hopped on behind him. She snuggled in and wrapped her arms around his torso. His body was warm. His shirt was untucked and she moved her hands under his shirt. She could tell he welcomed her touch. She loved the way he felt. She loved snuggling close to him. It made her feel safe.

She had forgotten how much she liked riding on a motorcycle. One summer after high school she had dated a guy with a bike. They were two crazy kids back then. They didn't wear helmets and she knew he drove way too fast. But she loved the way the wind felt on her face and blew through her hair. They were young and thought they were invincible. She smiled as she thought of the memory.

Off on another adventure. Greg had become a very valued friend in her life. She wasn't quite sure how or when the friendship had become so solid. "Hard wired," as he had told her. She wondered if their relationship would ever be more than good friends. For now she was content just holding on and letting the moment take them to their next destination.

The ride ended much too quickly and soon Greg was pulling into the drive that led to the farm. He parked the bike and he took off his helmet. She followed suit. "Got your hiking shoes on?" he asked as he hopped off the bike and helped her off.

"I've got my running shoes on." She smiled. "Just in case I get chased."

"Ha," he snickered. "Let me show you around before it gets totally dark. Come on." He grabbed her hand and led her to a clearing.

"That's the field my great-grandpa, my grandpa and my father plowed," he said with pride as his free outstretched hand swept the horizon. She squeezed his hand and smiled at him. She understood that kind of history. They walked further past the clearing and he showed her the idle acres by the river.

"It's getting dark. We better get back to the campsite and get the fire going." It wasn't long until she saw the campsite and ran ahead of him.

"Catch me if you can," she laughed.

"You're in trouble now," he replied. "My legs are a whole lot longer than yours." He quickly caught up to her and grabbed her. He turned her around gently took her face in his hands. He leaned over and gently kissed her lips. "You do make my heart race in your skin tight jeans," he whispered in her ear. She stroked his face and smiled.

"Let's build that fire," she said as she pulled away. It was hard to breathe. She shut her eyes and took a deep breath. Her head was spinning. She wanted to follow her heart. She didn't want to be the practical, good girl she had been taught to be all her life. The heart wanted what the heart wanted. But there was nagging doubt and uncertainty.

She helped him gather wood and kindling. She watched him stack and assemble the wood just so. Soon there was a cozy fire crackling away. She snuggled up next to him and enjoyed the warmth of the fire. She loved the way a campfire smelled. She could feel him starting to settle in. To his surprise, Tess suddenly hopped up and announced she had a surprise for him.

She didn't know if he would remember but she needed to know if he did. She grabbed her phone from her back pocket and clicked on the bookmark. A soft melody soon filled the quiet night air.

A CHANGED REFLECTION

"Hey, have you ever tried really reaching out for the other side…" She slowly turned to him. "You promised me a dance," she said with a smile.

"I can't dance worth a shit unless I have someone that can follow and stay with me," he replied.

"I promise, I'll stay with you." She smiled.

She started the song over. "I know that song. *Bread*. I think we may have even danced to that one once." He grabbed her and held her close.

"Yes, we did," she replied as she smiled and gazed up into his eyes. "And at the end of the evening you took me home with you," she whispered. He hugged her tighter.

Then he stopped and took her face in his hands. "Oh yeah, I DO remember that night," he said softly, smiling back at her. "You were beautiful. You still are Tess."

Chapter Sixteen

---※---

Tess penned a few more lines in her notebook. The one she kept her secrets in—her hopes, her insecurities. Then she carefully put it in her bag and quietly sat looking out the study hall windows.

The girls at the nearby table were starting to talk about prom. Where would they go to find the perfect dress and shoes? They would have to make a trip to the city. Tess could hear Lisa talking about who they should get to do their hair and nails? Would their dates get the perfect tux? Maggie wondered out loud if the tuxes their dates were getting would be good enough.

It was her senior prom. Tess hadn't gone her junior year. In fact, she had only been to one dance her entire high school existence: sophomore year homecoming, after much pleading. Todd didn't like to dance. He had even made her buy her own flower. She was so humiliated. She never talked about going to another dance again.

Tess knew in her heart Todd was not the one she wanted taking her to the last dance of her high school career. But this was senior prom. The theme was Stairway to Heaven. She had agreed to help with the decorations. She could make sure it would be a magical night for someone. She wondered if she could somehow find her own little piece of heaven.

Jim had gotten tired of Todd hassling him and had ended their relationship. Even though that relationship had come to a close, it had started a change in her. She knew she would never be quite the same. She was just beginning to understand that perhaps she did have something to offer. The problem was no one wanted to give her a chance to find out. She really wanted to go to prom. She wanted it to be special and she knew what her heart wanted. But sometimes it was easier to settle.

Todd was waiting at her locker and he was persistent. "Tess, please. Give me another chance. I know you really want to go to prom. Let me take you. I'll promise you I'll make the night special for you." He gently rubbed her shoulders and nuzzled his face into the side of her neck and kissed her softly. It was a public display of affection. An unknown to her and extremely unusual for him. She felt the tingling starting. Damn, she needed it.

Maybe this time would be different, Tess thought. She wanted it to be different. She wanted the Todd she had fallen in love with in junior high. Or did she just want the fantasy of someone who truly loved her and could rock her world like he knew how to do. He was an addiction she didn't know how to kick. She knew better but she finally caved. "Alright."

"So can I take you out tonight?" he asked as he wrapped his arms around her. She turned and looked into his blue eyes and smiled at him. "I suppose."

The butterflies churned. She knew what that would mean. It had been five months since she had been with him. Maybe he needed her as much as she needed him. It was the reason she kept letting him back into her world. A desire that was too complicated to control. She needed to feel his touch on her body. He hugged her and walked away to class. She immediately felt a pang of doubt.

She slowly closed her locker. Her emotions were conflicted. She was happy to have a date for prom. She knew he would fulfill a need. Her hopes of Greg taking her to prom had been dashed earlier in the day. He had asked Lisa Hanson. She wondered if there would ever be anything between them. She sighed. She guessed she would never know.

Her parents were less than delighted when she told them who her date for prom was and that they would be going out that night. Her mother was fairly vocal about it. Her father didn't say a word. But his look told her everything she needed to know. Her heart sank. More than anything in the world she hated to disappoint her father. She knew it would not be the night to be late for her curfew.

In the weeks that followed, Tess took road trips to start shopping for her perfect dress. She wanted something special but she was also very conscious about not spending too much. It was a value her parents had instilled in her. She had become a great bargain shopper. She finally found a long white dress accented with lace that had a plunging neckline. It would fit the fantasy of what prom should be. She truly was a hopeless romantic.

In the weeks leading up to prom she worked on her tan. She had the perfect place on the second floor porch of the farmhouse. She could lay out topless and no one would see her. It was a perfect way to get a golden tan without lines. She tanned nicely, thanks to her great-grandma MEME, and it would only make the neckline of her white dress that much more amazing. She might not be going to prom with Greg but she knew she would at least get his attention that night, if even for a moment.

To her surprise, Todd asked her about her dress because he said he wanted to get her the perfect flowers. Perhaps she would actually get her "stairway to heaven" after all. Prom day finally arrived. The school was buzzing. She helped with the last minute decorations in the gym before she headed home to start getting ready. She felt oddly content. It was a feeling she didn't have very often. She decided to enjoy it while it lasted.

Tess wanted to draw a bubble bath but realized she wouldn't have time to make it worthwhile so she opted for a shower. After her shower she started to get dressed. She had gotten a new white lace bra and panties to wear under her dress. She loved pretty lingerie. It always made her feel special. She took the dress from the closet and carefully put it on and looked in the mirror. She felt like Cinderella. She sat down at her vanity and brushed her long hair. The girl in the mirror seemed content with the reflection. That was an unusual occurrence.

"Tess, Todd is here," her mother hollered up the stairs.

"Okay, Mom. I'll be right there." She looked at herself one last time in the mirror. *This could be my wedding dress*, she thought. After she had given herself to him, she had always thought that the two of

A CHANGED REFLECTION

them would be together in the end. That they would spend their life together. Now she wasn't so sure, but tonight it didn't matter.

Tess lifted up the side of her dress and descended the stairs carefully. He was waiting for her in the living room. He had purchased an enormous bouquet filled with red and pink roses for her. He looked handsome in his tux. "You look really pretty Tess," he said as he smiled at her. Her mother had the camera. She wanted to take pictures. Her father was in the fields.

Timing was everything in a farmer's world. Tess understood that. It was a world she loved. Todd often complained about it to her. He didn't understand why she couldn't just work in the kitchen with her mother rather than in the fields with her father. Tess was happy her father wanted her driving the tractor in the fields. It was a way she could make him proud of her. She also loved being able to listen to music in the cab of the tractor. It was her special time.

Todd had borrowed his brother's car. When they got to the car he opened the car door for her. "You really do look beautiful, Tess," he told her as he snuck a kiss before she climbed into the car. *Maybe he really had changed*, she thought as they headed out the driveway.

They scooped the loop a couple of times before they got to the school. The gym looked spectacular. They had their picture taken in the swing that was inside the gates to the "stairway to heaven." Tess felt like she was in heaven. At least at first.

As the evening wore on, Tess started to question her decision to take Todd back. With each slow dance the body language between the two of them became more strained. Finally Tess told Todd she needed some fresh air.

He followed her outside and reached into his pocket and grabbed a cigarette. She looked at him with a frown. Todd knew she didn't like smoking. He lit up and then told her it was her fault for all the stress she had caused.

She looked at him with astonishment. "I can't believe you're telling me that the reason you've started smoking is MY fault. I've caused YOU stress?" Tess glared at Todd in disbelief. "Are you kidding me, Todd?" She turned and went back inside to the gym. He followed her and grabbed her by the arm. She wanted to push him away but didn't want to make a scene at the school.

"Come on, Tess. You wanted to dance. This is the last one." He grabbed her wrist so tightly that she winced. It wasn't the first time. She could feel the rage inside her start to grow. Damn him. She had been kidding herself. The last song was "Stairway to Heaven." He put his arms around her. She bristled but did not fight him. She just went through the motions. She closed her eyes and started listening to the words as she often did.

> Yes, there are two paths you can go by, but in the long run
> There's still time to change the road you're on.
> And it makes me wonder.

Two paths. Perhaps she was heading down the wrong one and needed to make a change. She was beginning to wonder.

Chapter Seventeen

---※---

Tess felt a sense of accomplishment as she made the last swipe across the yard with the mower. It was a great day. She smiled as she thought of Greg. He had shared something very special and personal with her. He teased her and kidded with her but she had come to realize he had a very serious and private side to him. There were certain things Greg was guarded about and was cautious in sharing. The farm was one of them. He had shared some of his family history with her. She knew that was a decision he had not taken lightly. She thought about what he had said to her that night about the farm. "I belong to it."

She had grown up on a farm. She had always thought he was a city boy. When he had made the remark to her, she understood. The land got under your skin. It might be something you could own, but for certain people, even if you left and walked away, it was always a part of you. It would always call you home. She was discovering that was true for her. She had never dreamed that this was something they shared in common.

Tess sat on the bed and started to sort through the box of old photographs her mother had meticulously preserved. She smiled as she came across the big glossy photo of her father in the milking parlor. She had loved the sounds and smells of the milking parlor as a little girl. There was nothing like the fresh clean smell of chlorine or the rhythmic sounds of the milkers. Once in a while a sound or smell would trigger those memories. It made her sad that the milking parlor was slowly falling apart. "Someone will bulldoze it down before long," her father had told her on her last trip to the farm.

She remembered her father's dairy herd of Holsteins. She marveled at how he had named and remembered the entire herd. They all had numbered ear tags, but he had called them all by name and they responded to him. He gave all the animals on the farm names, even strays. He often gave regular visitors nicknames too, although they weren't always politically correct. It was one of the things that endeared him to her.

When she was very young, her father would take her brother and her with him on trips to Wisconsin for dairy auctions. They would take a small four passenger plane. She loved those trips. She would look with wonder out the plane window at the ground below. It looked like a huge green patchwork quilt. Little did she realize she would observe the same view without a plane with her cousin Cat years later. Perhaps that was when she realized her love of flying and soaring above the earth.

When they would arrive at the auction, her father would take them to a massive tent where the auctioneers would be busy calling out the bids. It had fascinated her. There were hundreds of men like her father vying for a chance to get that special black and white beauty. The auctioneer would talk a mile a minute and she would listen to the constant sound of "Yep, yep" as the bidding went up. Then there would be a smack of a gavel and the auctioneer would shout "SOLD!" It was a cherished memory.

As she thought of the cows, she could almost smell the aroma of fresh cut alfalfa and she instantly thought of the hay mow. The big old barn was gone now but her smile widened as she remembered her brother building the amazing forts and tunnels in that hay mow. It was an engineering marvel. To her he was a genius. There were dozens of tunnels connecting rooms all across the barn. Each room was complete with seating for several. They would spend hours playing in the hay mow. It was another memory etched forever in her mind.

She loved her brother. She seldom said it, but she knew he knew. It was a Carrington thing. Outsiders didn't always understand. She also knew he always had her back and always would. Nothing came before family.

Suddenly the smile left her face. It was in that hay mow where she experienced her first life altering event. She was in second grade. Her mother was covering up the opening where the hay bales came into the hay mow because the weather had turned cold. Her brother was going to have a church Halloween party. As was typical of her mother, she didn't take time to get a ladder, she just climbed up on the little ledges on the side of the barn wall. With the last hammer of the nail, she lost her balance and fell the 15 feet to the floor of the hay mow.

Tess knew instantly her mother was hurt badly. She didn't remember her mother crying, only giving her brother and her instructions on what to do in a very strained and altered voice. Her father was in the field. There were no cell phones in those days. Her mother had crawled across the floor of the hay mow and climbed down the wooden rung ladder on her hands and knees. It was the only way to get out of the hay mow.

Her mother had instructed her brother to get the lawn mower and attach the cart they often used to pick up sticks and other yard waste from the farm so he could get her to the house. She instructed Tess to run to the house to call her grandmother who lived in town and tell her what had happened quickly and ask her to call the ambulance. Tess remembered thinking her mother was going to die.

Her mother had been in great pain, but she mopped the kitchen floor on her hands and knees while she waited for the ambulance. Tess remembered watching the ambulance taking her mother away. She thought she was going away forever. Her mother had crushed both her ankles. She had later asked her mother why she mopped the floor that night. She had told her it was a way to keep her mind off the pain. Her mother was the rock of the family. That was the beginning of learning the lesson to "suck it up."

She taught me that lesson well, thought Tess sadly.

She knew life had come full circle when her mother died. She had been in Minneapolis when her father had called to tell her that her mother was gone. After a frantic two hour drive to the farm she was greeted by her father. He looked at her and said, "Good, now you can take care of things." She had become the rock. There was no time to grieve. There were things to be taken care of.

Tess always felt like she was different. She never felt like she quite fit in with the town kids growing up. She didn't have next door neighbors to play with. She learned to fill her time with imagination and her surroundings. She learned to appreciate little things like finding where the momma cat had hidden her kittens or letting a young calf suck on her fingers.

Tess knew that the farm had always held a special place for her. It was something that no one could ever take from her. It was a part of her. Her brother had moved away but she could never stray too far. Greg was right. She belonged to it too.

Chapter Eighteen

Calvin and his crew had done a remarkable job. In one day they had replaced all the outside doors of the lake house. They had cleaned up their mess and left no signs they had even been there. The snow had taken its toll on the doors over the years with no one to scoop away the drifts in the winter. Someday she would change that.

Tess had taken a chance when she asked Calvin for his help. Everyone had told her he was the best but that there would be no way she could get his help on short notice. He was booked for months. Like so many things in her life, she did things on the spur of the moment. So she took a chance and asked him anyway. The worst he could say to her was no. She was thrilled when he had agreed to come do the work with so little notice.

She was thankful that he had agreed to come back and hang the outside canvas curtain on her porch for her. Had she known the company who made the replacement curtain wouldn't hang the new one, she would have gone elsewhere. When the company had put the grommets in the wrong places she was beside herself. Calvin had looked at it and told her he would be glad to take care of it. "That's what friends are for, Tess. It's really no big deal." To her it was huge.

Now Tess had to begin the monumental task of getting everything repainted. It would have been easier just to paint everything one color, but she just couldn't quite bring herself to change the color scheme her mother had created years before. The lake house was her last real connection to her mother. She knew why her mother loved the lake so much. She felt her presence there.

She was glad she was alone and didn't have to deal with painting drama. Painting was therapeutic for her. There was something about the way the paint brush touched the wood and then glided across it, transforming it. As the day wore on and her water bottle ran dry, Tess realized she was totally covered with paint. No one had ever said she was a neat and tidy painter, but she got the job done. And after all, she was a creative person. She was supposed to be messy.

Suddenly she was tired. She had hit the proverbial brick wall. Rather than track through the house, she decided to take a shower in the guesthouse. It didn't require climbing stairs and the shower was bigger than the one in the big house. Plus, she could give it a cleaning at the same time. Multitasking was the name of the game these days.

Tess opened the screen door and decided to open up a couple of the windows to help cool off the little house. None of the neighbors were around so she didn't worry about stripping down to nothing in the middle of the room. She left her pile of clothes on the floor. She looked at it and laughed. "I could have been the wicked witch and simply melted," she said to herself. She would pick up her clothes once she was all cleaned up.

She left the door to the bathroom wide open since there were no windows or exhaust fan. She just knew she was hot and tired and a cool shower would feel good. She had washed the rug she kept on the tiles outside the shower, but it was hanging on the line, and she didn't want to put her clothes back on to get it. She would just use her towel as a bath mat after she dried off.

She turned the handles and started the water. She knew she had to let it run for a while, or the water would be freezing since the warm water came from the big house. She had learned that lesson the hard way. After what seemed liked forever, she felt the water finally get hot.

Tess stepped into the shower and made a mental note exactly where the soap and shampoo were. These things were important to know when your eyes were closed and full of suds. She slowly began her ritual. She closed her eyes and put her head back. She let the water run down her face and body. She ran her hands through her

A CHANGED REFLECTION

hair until it was completely wet. She brushed the water out of her face one last time before she grabbed the shampoo.

Tess squeezed a blob of shampoo onto her palm, closed her eyes again, and started slowly massaging the shampoo into her hair. She kept her eyes closed tightly so she wouldn't get soap in them. She had been listening to Chicago while she was painting, and the last song was repeating in her head. She started to sing, *"When I'm with you, doesn't matter where we are…"*

She stopped. She thought she had heard the screen door open. She waited. Nothing. She continued to sing, *"I'm with you. That's all that matters…"*

"Oh really? Tell me more," she heard the familiar deep voice say from the other room. Oh my god. He was there, and she was only a few feet away stark naked.

"What are you doing here?" she asked, trying not to sound nervous. She had no clean clothes in the bathroom, and the door was wide open.

"I met some friends for lunch and thought I'd check to see if you were here. Obviously you are. I'll just wait while you finish your shower. I have a towel here I can wrap you in 'my pretty' since it looks like the wicked witch melted on the floor out here."

"Sorry about that. I was going to pick them up when I was done. I'll try to be quick." She giggled nervously. She hated the fact that he made her so nervous. He was just a good friend, and they had had some history, but things were too complicated for it to be anything else at the moment.

"Take your time, Tess. I'm not in a hurry." She tried to decipher the tone of his voice, but the hot water quickly put her back in the "I don't give a shit" mode, and she went back to her business.

She continued to massage the shampoo into her hair. She grabbed the loofah and squeezed some body soap onto it. She squeezed it between her fingers until she felt the lather explode. She slowly drug the loofah up one arm and then down the other. Then she started at her toes and worked her way up her legs and inner thighs. She loved the way soap was so slippery and tickled her body.

She completed her ritual by slowly rubbing the loofah across her breasts. She put her head under the water and let it wash away all the soap from her eyes. When she finally opened them, she turned to see his smiling face looking at her. He had been watching her. "So did you enjoy the show?" she asked him.

"Oh yeah," he said with a huge grin on his face.

"Well, you'll have to pay admission." She grabbed his shirt and pulled him into the shower. He laughed and pushed her back against the wall of the shower and kissed her. Tess forgot that she had nothing on and kissed him back with the same intensity. She paused only long enough to grab his shirt and rip the buttons off it and pull the soaking piece of cloth from his body. Then she noticed that it was the only piece of clothing he had on.

"Sorry about that," she said breathlessly, "but you started this. And I'm going to make sure you finish it." She grinned.

"If I must." He winked at her. "But, Tess, the door and windows are wide open. So you can't utter a word. Promise me. Not one sound."

He knew from the past that this request was next to impossible for Tess. He delighted in knowing he could make her squirm and she had to keep quiet. He started to run his hand along her sides and cupped her breasts in each hand. "They're so beautiful." He leaned over and kissed them gently and then started sucking on her nipples. She started to gulp in air.

"Not a word. You promised," he whispered in her ear and then started to kiss her down her neck.

His hands found their way down her sides and between her legs. He was exploring everywhere with his fingers. He could tell she was losing control. He kissed her lips and then whispered in her ears. "Shhhh." He was delighting in the fact she was taking great pleasure but couldn't utter a sound.

When he thought she was about to burst he grabbed her ass, lifted her up, and pushed inside her. "Why are you biting your lip with your eyes closed, Tess?" he asked with a smile. Keeping quiet was making her head pound. "Is there something you want to say?"

"Is there something you want to say?" Greg asked her again.

Tess slowly opened her eyes. She was wrapped in a towel on the bathroom floor. How had she gotten here?

"I don't understand..." she started to say. Her head was pounding. She tried hard to focus. It took her a moment to get her bearings.

"Best I can tell is that you slipped and hit your head getting out of the shower. That's quite a bump you have on your noggin. Good thing I decided to stop by. You might have been lying here awhile. I guess you came by the nickname of Grace honestly." He smiled. She felt her face redden.

"I'm just glad you're not hurt," he said.

Nothing but my ego, she thought.

"You do look pretty nice in just your towel though." He laughed.

Her mind was foggy as she looked at him.

"Let me help you up. I didn't want to move you until you came to. I was just about ready to call 911."

Greg gently slipped his arm around her and helped her onto the couch. "Are you sure you're okay?" he asked quietly.

"Yes, I'll be fine. It's just that..." She couldn't tell him what had just happened in her head. He would think she was crazy.

He smiled at her as if he knew exactly what had been going on in her head.

Chapter Nineteen

It was another Friday night at home. Her parents had gone out. Tess was in the big old farm house alone. Alone. Not a new concept for her. Something she often felt even when she was surrounded by people. The feeling seemed to follow her. It had for a long time. She wondered if it would ever go away.

Tess headed to the kitchen and searched the lazy Susan until she found just the right pan. It would be a perfect night for popcorn. Her grandmother had taught her how to make it when she was very little. She adored her grandmother. She wanted to be strong and independent like her someday. Her grandmother told her stories about her great-great-grandmother MEME. Another incredibly strong woman.

Tess often found herself daydreaming about MEME. Someday she would go to Barbados and try to find more about her. She would research the Edingales who had shunned her. All of them, making her life unbearable, except for her great-great-grandfather Thomas who had loved her dearly until his untimely death. He was the reason she stayed. And true to his word, he had left his entire family fortune to her when he died in an ironclad will.

When she was in grade school she always looked forward to those special Saturday nights when she would get to stay overnight at her grandmother's house. Her grandmother would bring out the heavy metal pan, add a little oil and let it get sizzling hot. Then she would pour in some popcorn and put the lid on and wait for the popping to start.

As the corn would pop, her grandmother would quickly slide the pan across the burner to stir the popcorn so it wouldn't burn. It was a rare occasion when her grandmother would burn a batch of corn. Once the popping stopped, her grandmother would dump the freshly popped corn into a large metal bowl and drizzle it with rich creamy butter. Her grandmother would give her her own bowl and would let her fill it as many times as she wanted.

Once the corn was popped and in the bowl, her grandmother would send her to the back porch to grab a couple of bottles of 7Up. Tess didn't have soda pop growing up, so it was an extra special treat. The neighbor lady would come over and the ladies would settle in the two comfy chairs and Tess would plop on the floor with a pillow and they would all watch *The Lawrence Welk Show*.

As the corn started popping, Tess smiled and spun around the kitchen pretending she was Sissy. Waiting for Bobby to grab her hand. The moment didn't last long because even though a watched pot never boils, an unwatched pan often burns.

Once the popcorn was in the bowl, she grabbed an apple and sliced it in quarters. She grabbed a diet Pepsi and headed to the den. She knew there would be a Hallmark movie on and she knew that at least one girl would find happiness.

Two hours and several Kleenex later, the girl ended up with the guy and all was well in the world. At least the world of make believe. Tess was an expert in the world of the imaginary. It was often how she survived her loneliness.

She picked up her dishes and took them to the kitchen. Once everything was loaded into the dishwasher and thrown into the trash, she flipped off the top light and headed up the stairs. *These stairs*, she thought. Stairs that would take her to her room in the castle. Her prison of sorts, but where she felt safe and secure. A place where no one could hurt her. A place where she was beautiful. A place where she was enough.

She navigated the hallway in the dark, turned the corner and felt for the light switch in her room. Her books were staring at her. She had brought them home with her. She was ahead on her assignments but doing school work was sometimes a good distraction. She might not have a social life but she certainly could have a scholastic one.

She reached for her journal and favorite pen and plopped down on her bed. Once more she would fill another page with feelings. When she had finished, she dated her entry and closed the journal. If only closing the cover could close the chapter of her life she was living. Tomorrow she could open it and begin a new chapter. A happier one with the smiling face from her homeroom.

She got up off her bed and put her journal back in its special place. Her eye caught the corner of her most recent acceptance letter. She knew she had the grades to get accepted to almost any school in the country. She sighed. She had applied to only two and had now been accepted to both.

She had chosen a good university, but it was not where her heart truly wanted to go. Once again, she realized her decisions were being affected by others, including Todd. Why couldn't she break free and fly away? Why didn't she have the courage to truly believe in herself and go out and find the world she was truly meant to live in?

She was not following her dreams. They would not pay the bills. That dream was not a "sustainable" career. Tess touched her journal once more. This journal was her security and lifeblood. Without it, she was not sure she would survive. It was where she shared her innermost thoughts and secrets. It was where her pleas for help were penned. This journal and dreams in the night from grandma MEME were what saved her.

A sudden sadness filled Tess. She was thinking of her friend Linda. The two had been close friends in grade school and junior high. Tess had pulled away from all her friends the past three years. She had been consumed by her own sadness and self-doubt. Now she would have to find a way to forgive herself for not being the kind of friend Linda needed the past year. If she had, perhaps they would be celebrating their graduation together.

Instead, she had helped Linda's distraught mother plan a funeral. No one had seen Linda's pleas for help, just like they hadn't seen hers. But Tess knew Linda was not as strong. Tess knew Linda didn't have a grandmother MEME guiding her in her dreams or a cousin like Cat who always seemed to be there at just the right time. Cat constantly reminded her that she was in no way to blame for her friend's death.

A CHANGED REFLECTION

Tess turned and grabbed an album from the stack on her floor. She gently put it on the spindle, taking care not to scratch it. *This one seems appropriate*, she thought. She lit a candle by her bed, grabbed her pillow, and then turned off the lights in her room. She started to slowly dance around her room to the beat of the music. She closed her eyes, squeezed the pillow as if it were human and sang along to the words. She knew them by heart.

> Tell me what's wrong with you now,
> Tell me why I …
> Never seem to make you happy
> Though heaven knows I try.
> What does it take to please you?
> Tell me just how…
> Break up to make up
> That's all we do.
> First you love me, then you hate me,
> That's a game for fools.

Tears were falling onto the pillow. She held it close, hoping somehow it might hug her back.

She was so tired of the game. She wanted to walk away. She knew she needed to and every time she tried the passion sucked her back in. Someday she would find the passion without all the hurt. She needed to believe that. She would one day softly speak the words "Is it you?" just as the character in the book she had just read had done.

She went to her dresser and opened the top drawer. This would make her feel better. It was a turquoise lacy baby doll nightie. The color of the Caribbean. Water. Her happy place. Someday she would go to Barbados to see where great-great-grandma MEME was born. That thought brought a smile to her face. She shed her clothes and slipped into the nightie.

She lit the candles on her vanity and sat down. She opened the drawer, grabbed her brush and began brushing her long golden-brown hair. She studied the girl in the mirror looking back at her. Not beautiful, but maybe pretty enough.

A new song. She smiled and began singing along once again with the *Stylistics*.

> There's a spark of magic in your eyes,
> Candyland appears each time you smile.

His smile made her heart flutter. She could dream. Graduation was just around the corner and who knew what might happen after that. Why hadn't she tried to tell Greg the way she felt when she had the chance? She knew. If she did and he didn't feel the same she would be devastated. If she never told him, he could never reject her.

Someday. Somewhere. She would get her chance to show him what he meant to her. She would take the risk because she knew in her heart it was the right thing. She didn't know why his smile always made her heart skip a beat. But one day she would make his heart skip a beat too.

For tonight she could close her eyes and pretend he was holding her close while they danced. Her head resting on his chest. She could hear his heartbeat. She felt safe with his arms around her. As long as the music played, her dream was real.

Betcha by golly wow. You're the one…

Chapter Twenty

The screaming had to stop. The constant fear of living on the edge not knowing what might cause it to start again was becoming too much. Something had to give. She felt as if she were on a sinking ship and she was trying desperately to find her way out. If she stayed she would surely drown. If she tried to leave... She shuddered at the thought.

Tess knew things were complicated. She also knew she couldn't ignore it anymore. Whatever "it" was or was becoming. Her life was being sucked out of her. It didn't seem to matter. The "good girl guilt" was overwhelming. Its gripes were dug deeply into her soul. She so wished she had the strength and fortitude of her grandmother MEME.

How had she survived the fury and wrath of the Edingales? Tess smiled. It was her great-great-grandfather Thomas. The love of her life and she was the love of his. A love so special and so rare. Their love and passion was what Tess was holding out for. She believed it was out there. Somewhere in time. She would find it.

She headed to the garage. Full of stuff, like her life. Stuff that needed to be sorted out, tossed or placed high on a shelf as a memory to be retrieved from time to time. Before she began the daunting task of cleaning out the garage she took out her phone and posted about what her "exciting afternoon adventure" was going to be.

Sometimes she posted things just to see if he would notice and "like" them. It was her way of knowing that at least for a moment he was thinking about her too. Five minutes later he responded with a comment. "Get away from there."

Yes, she thought, *I would love to get away from here and be with you.* But life was not that simple. She closed her eyes and thought back to a simpler time. Crawling through forts her brother had made in the hay mow. Swinging from the rope swing and dropping into a pile of hay. Laughing. If only things were that simple now. It was the laughter she missed most of all.

She searched for the old radio that had been in the garage. At least if she had to endure this arduous task she could have her music. What seemed like an hour later, she found it buried under a pile of gardening tools. She had loved to garden. She had loved to do a lot of things but that had changed. Her world had changed.

She gently laid the gardening tools aside and dusted off the radio and plugged it in. She turned it on and scrolled through the static until she found a station that came in clearly. Immediately the words caught her attention and she started listening to the song she knew she had heard before. This time it was different.

> I'm caught up in this moment, caught up in your smile
> I've never opened up to anyone.

Ironic. Truer words could not have been spoken at that moment. His smile had always made her feel warm all over. Ever since junior high. She had snapped a photo of him at her junior high party. He had that wonderful smile on his face. She still had the photo and took it out and looked at it from time to time. She wasn't quite sure why she had kept it.

As she thought of him she realized she had shared things with him she hadn't shared with anyone before. She knew she had his friendship even if her heart was holding out for so much more.

We don't need to rush this. Let's just take it slow.

"I consider you one of my oldest and dearest friends," he had told her. "But I really don't know you very well." She knew she needed to get to know him better. She needed to get inside his head like he had gotten into hers. She needed to know what had really prompted him to come see her at the beginning of the summer. Why had he sent her a text that he would stop and visit her sometime? There was something there. Tess just didn't know what.

> And I don't want to mess this thing up
> No, I don't want to push too far
> Just a shot in the dark that you just might
> Be the one I've been waiting for my whole life.

A shot in the dark. Perhaps. She knew there was only one way to find out for sure. But did she have the courage and strength to find out? She sat down on the stool she had cleared off. She looked around the garage. She felt overwhelmed. She felt just like she did in high school. She was screaming for help but why didn't anyone see? And if they did, would it make any difference now?

Then she heard the melodic voice in her head. "It's you. It's always been you."

She smiled. MEME. "Yes, MEME," she whispered. "You're right. Courage comes from within, not from anyone else. I have to find the courage and be strong like you were." A warm breeze brushed her face. "Thank you."

She started sifting through the boxes. Old papers that needed to be shredded. Pictures from a friend's birthday party. Then she saw it. The journal she had kept in high school. She picked it up and slowly turned the pages. She read the words she had written so long ago.

> Please leave me alone.
> Don't come near—
> You may come too close.
> And I might see a person.
> Then it would start
> All over again—
> I would begin to care,
> And put you first.
> Slowly I might even fall in love,
> Only to be let down
> And hurt greatly.
> I can't take it anymore!

So please—
Just leave me alone.

So much hurt. So much loneliness. The hurt had faded but the memories were still very clear. Reminding her. She had put up walls to never let that kind of hurt in again. Walls that she had never totally taken down. Walls that kept her from really feeling. Walls that kept her heart safe. Walls that left her lonely.

Tears started to well up in her eyes. It took her back to a time when she had tried desperately to forget the hurt but could not forget the passion. A passion she kept searching for but had eluded her. And now, even though she was surrounded by people in her life she felt utterly, totally alone and sad.

Some days the sadness overwhelmed her and made her heart ache. She was the caregiver for everyone else and there was nothing left for her. She was always the good girl. Doing what was expected of her, doing what everyone else thought she should do. She wondered if she would ever be able to truly follow her heart. Would she ever find true happiness and that passion she so longed for?

As she closed the cover of the journal another *Lady Antebellum* tune came on the radio. She liked listening to them. She started listening to the words as she always did.

> Every heartache makes you stronger
> But it won't be much longer
> You'll find love, you'll find peace
> And the you you're meant to be
> I know right now that's not the way you feel
> But one day you will.

She stood up and bumped the pile in front of her. She jumped back just in time to avoid being hit by an avalanche of boxes. "Damn it," she said with disgust. She kicked the box closest to her. It all needed to go away. Everything. "I am so done with this mess. I have to find a way out," she muttered. She heaved a heavy sigh.

She sat back down on the stool and closed her eyes. How could she possibly do this? Where would she find the strength? The sweet voice once again reminded her. "It's you. It's always been you. Carrington women never give up and never give in. No one said life would ever be easy. But I'll always be here for you."

"I know," she whispered with a smile. She knew in her heart great-great-grandma MEME was always with her and was carefully watching over her.

Chapter Twenty-One

She needed time away. She had to do some serious thinking. Something had to change. She remembered the psychologist she had seen years before at her mother's request. She had told her that the tolerance level of humans was measured on a scale of 1–10. Many people live at a very unhappy state of 9.99. But until the line has been crossed and 10 is reached, people don't change. People were creatures of habit. The scales were tipping.

Tess browsed through her closet. She wondered what she should wear. She had finally decided it would be good to go to her cousin's wedding in Chicago. She could see her mother's side of the family. The last time she had seen most of them was at her uncle's funeral. This would be a much happier time. Family was important to her. It became an easy decision.

As she perused her closet she came across the sleeveless black and white dress with the matching jacket. It had properly placed sequins to give it just a bit of sparkle and it showed off her cleavage quite nicely. She had been feeling down and the dress made her feel good. She had only worn it once before to the gala.

She had worked hard on that gala. Her friend Denny was the driving force. He gave of himself tirelessly and had inspired so many others. Now he was gone. It was still so hard to believe. So suddenly and without warning. It made her realize how short and precious life really was. No one really knew how much time they had.

Denny had asked her to be one of the opening speakers. She had stood up in front of 1,000 people and told them her story. The pain of remembering that story was excruciating but she did not cry. She had felt her mother's spirit and strength with her that night.

She hung the dress on the closet door. She sat on the bedroom floor in front of her closet to look at her shoe collection to decide what she could wear. She opted for her cute black heels. She figured she would be sitting at the wedding most of the time anyway, so why not wear shoes that would make her legs look good. That thought made her smile. One of guys she had worked with at a previous job had told her she had a well turned ankle.

She went to her jewelry box to pick out the perfect pieces. She chose a sterling and CZ set with a design incorporated to make them look like tiny sparkly presents. She had given herself this present after a season of hard work on the jewelry circuit. They were simple but stunning pieces. They would accent the dress nicely. She packed them in her jewelry pouch and tucked them into her suitcase.

The weekend in Chicago would provide her with some alone time she needed. She had some serious thinking to do away from the drama. Things got more complicated with each passing day. She was repeating high school—putting on a facade of happiness that everything was okay. She was coming to the realization that she had been living a life for someone else. It was finally her time. The worst part about being strong was that no one ever asked her if she was okay. She was looking forward to finding the spa and taking advantage of room service.

She finished packing her suitcase making sure she had her special bag and her bubble bath. She grabbed a water and headed out the door. She gave her dogs both big hugs. They hated it when she was gone. Her daughter had told her that Lilly pouted when she was away. Lilly knew she wasn't going to get to go and headed back to the bedroom. Except for her dogs, Tess realized she was happier when she was away than when she was at home. She put her suitcase in the trunk and backed down the driveway.

She loved driving by herself. It was her thinking and reflecting time. It was the time she could spend with her music. It was her time and nothing could take it away from her. She could get lost in the music and her memories and dreams. She started thinking of him and the William Faulkner quote he had posted. "Memory believes before knowing remembers. Believes longer than recollects, longer than knowing even wonders." The memories she had of him sometimes consumed her and still caused her heart to flutter.

Memories. She smiled as she remembered that special memory. That special night that he remembered too. Someday. Somewhere. She would add to it. She would have another memory with him. She felt it.

She put a Lady Antebellum disc into the CD player. She settled in and began her drive. She smiled and started singing along as the words to "One Day You Will" filled the car.

> You feel like you're falling backward
> Like you're slippin' through the cracks
> Like no one would even notice
> If you left this town and never came back
> You walk outside and all you see is rain
> You look inside and all you feel is pain
> And you can't see it now
> But down the road the sun is shining
> In every cloud there's a silver lining
> Just keep holding on
> And every heartache makes you stronger
> But it won't be much longer
> You'll find love, you'll find peace
> And the you you're meant to be
> I know right now that's not the way you feel
> But one day you will.

One day. She hoped so. She was glad it was Saturday morning and there wasn't much traffic to fight. She didn't understand how someone could tackle it every day. Today she wouldn't have to. She could enjoy the crystal blue sky and watching the farmers start their fall rituals.

She missed the farm. She paused the music for a moment. What if her grandmother had told HER she needed to come back to the farm and take over because the Carrington family farm tradition needed to continue? What if she hadn't felt compelled to find a husband to solve that dilemma? She couldn't dwell on the what-ifs. She knew her life would have been drastically different. It didn't matter. It was what it was.

She made good time. She pulled up to the doors of the hotel. She was going to treat herself all weekend. It would start with valet parking. She let the handsome young man take her bag from the trunk. She handed him the keys and a nice tip and she walked into the hotel. She turned slightly and he gave her a big smile. She was such a sucker for a cute guy with a great smile.

She finally checked in after a struggle searching through her bag for her wallet. She was delighted to find out they had decided to upgrade her room to a suite at no extra charge. The stay was starting out on a high note. Fourteenth floor. High enough to have a great view.

She unlocked the door and walked over to the windows while the porter brought in her luggage and placed it in her closet. Her room had a spectacular view of the city. She gave him a tip and he quickly left and she set her purse and notebook down on the table. She looked at the clock and decided she had better get started getting ready for Scott's wedding.

She headed to the closet and grabbed her black and white dress from the garment bag. "Good," she said to herself. "No wrinkles." She hung it on the hook of the bathroom door. She stripped off her clothes and hopped into the shower. This had to be quick so that she wouldn't be late for the wedding and reception. Later she would treat herself to the large Jacuzzi bath. She had brought her bubbles along just in case.

She wasted no time. She toweled herself off quickly. She took the powder puff and slid it across her body so that her black lace bra and panties went on with ease. She slipped into her dress. She felt good in it. She knew she looked good in it. It was all about presentation.

At the gala her girlfriend had told her she looked hot in the dress. She filled it out in all the right places and the plunging neckline showed off her cleavage. She remembered that night and feeling relieved after she had gotten through with her little speech.

She brushed her hair and added a little spray to keep the bangs out of her eyes. She took a little extra time with her makeup just to be sure she looked her best. She wanted to be the best looking cousin in the room. She added a touch of perfume.

She reached for her jewelry pouch and grabbed the set she had chosen and put on the necklace and earrings. She chose the teardrop CZ ring instead of the one that matched the necklace and earrings. It was the same one she had worn to the gala. It had hearts etched in the sides of the ring. It was the teardrop for her daughter, forever in her heart. She rubbed the surface of the teardrop and sadly smiled.

The wedding was short and sweet. The bride was beautiful. It was nice to see a couple so in love. The reception that followed was filled with laughter and memories of growing up. All the cousins were telling stories. After their grandmother had died, the family seldom got together—except for weddings and funerals. She spent extra time visiting with her aunt—her mother's sister. It was her last physical female connection to her mother. If she closed her eyes, she could hear her mother's voice when her aunt talked.

The evening passed quickly. It was getting late and the group was starting to disband. Tess decided to head to her room. There was still time for that bubble bath and she would be glad to get her shoes off. Cute shoes only lasted so long.

She found her way to the lobby and entered the elevator and started to reach for the button for her floor. Just as the doors were getting ready to close she heard men talking and then a man's voice call out. "Could you hold the elevator for us please?" Of course she would. But there was something about that voice.

She held the button to hold the door open. She was looking down at the newly acquired scuff on her shoes but when the men entered the elevator she looked up. Her eyes got wide and she let out a gasp as she dropped her evening purse. The older man picked up her evening purse and handed it to her, grasping her hand with both of his. There was the familiar smile. She couldn't utter a word. The elevator suddenly became very warm. She felt her heart start to beat quickly.

"Tess, I think this belongs to you," he said with a grin.

Chapter Twenty-Two

Her head was spinning and her heart was beating fast. She felt her palms become sweaty. "Thank you," was all she could utter out of her mouth. The elevator was filling up. They were pushed to the back of the elevator. She knew he was in town for a family wedding but what were the chances they were staying at the same hotel?

"Fourteen, please," she asked the young man who was closest to the door. The words barely came out. She studied his face briefly. There was something familiar about him. Before she could make the connection, Greg spoke to her again.

"So, Tess, what are YOU doing in Chicago?" He said with a smile as he quietly slipped his hand behind her. She could feel the pressure of his hand on her ass as he gently squeezed.

With all the control she could muster, she replied, "I came for my cousin's wedding. It was a last minute decision but something just told me I should come. I've learned to listen to my instincts."

She knew why he was in town but thought it was best not to acknowledge that information since she didn't know if perhaps some of the people in the elevator were part of his family. She opened her evening purse and felt for her room keys. The woman at check in had given her two keys. She had told her she only needed one.

The woman behind the desk had smiled at her and told her to keep the extra key. "You might lose one in that big bag of yours," she had said with a wink in her eye. She had brushed off the remark and hadn't given it a second thought. Until now.

She discreetly took one of the keys from her purse, slid her hand behind her and slipped it into the hand that was on her ass. "I think

A CHANGED REFLECTION

I've only seen you a couple of times since high school," she said with a smile. He took the key from her and pinched her ass slightly. He felt her twitch and smiled.

"It has been a long time, Tess. I think the last time might have been at a party at the club," he said with a grin. "I think I might have even danced with you." Her heart skipped a beat. *Yes, that night*, she thought as she tried desperately to keep her composure.

"I'm not sure about that, but I do remember watching you play football. You were number 18, right?" she asked with a wink of her eye. He laughed. "That was a long time ago." The elevator stopped. The young man turned to her, smiled, and said, "It's your floor, number 14." The smile. She instantly knew who he was. "It was good seeing you Greg," she said. Her breast brushed against him as she tried to maneuver out of the crowded elevator. Her heart was pounding.

"It was great to see you too. We should try to get together for coffee sometime." She could feel his eyes watching her as she was leaving the elevator. "And yes, I was number 18," he replied and winked at her as she exited.

She turned and replied, "I'd like that. Enjoy the rest of your evening." She eased out of the crowded elevator and walked slowly down the hall. She turned around one last time just as the elevator door was closing. She could see the smile on his face. He had taken the key. Did he understand her cryptic message? Time would tell. Like his words... que sera.

Tess headed down the hall until she reached 1418. She unlocked the door, slipped inside and closed it gently behind her and immediately took off her shoes. She set her evening bag down on the side table in the living room. She looked at herself in the full length mirror. Not so bad after all these years. She noticed a bottle of chilled champagne on the table and two glasses. Compliments of the hotel. The upgrade had come with a few perks. She hoped she would have the opportunity to share it.

She headed into the bedroom and dropped her shoes in the closet. She opened her suitcase and grabbed the black lace nightie and black satin robe. She noticed housekeeping had turned down the bed. She headed into the bathroom and started the water for her long awaited Jacuzzi bath. She added her bubbles and watched as the white foam started to accumulate.

She returned to the bedroom of her suite and slowly slipped out of her dress and hung it in the closet. She stripped out of her bra and panties and put them in the side zipper of her suitcase. She ran her hands slowly across the curves of her body. She smiled sadly. Naked and alone in a beautiful suite. Who had ever said life was fair. She grabbed her bottle of body lotion and laid it on the table by the sofa. After her bath she would massage some onto her legs. It always felt so good after a bath.

She grabbed her phone and scrolled until she found the Pandora app. It popped up with classic rock radio. She clicked on it and headed to her bubble bath. She stopped long enough to turn off the lights except for the one by the bedroom door. She set her phone down on the bathroom vanity, and slowly eased herself into the hot bath. It warmed her soul. It felt good. She sank down until her head was surrounded by bubbles. She closed her eyes and got lost in the music.

She wasn't sure exactly how long she had been soaking. A noise snapped her out of her trance. She opened her eyes and listened carefully. She heard the door click and slowly open and close. It was followed by the familiar sound of a deadbolt lock. "Hello?" She called out.

"Who were you expecting?" he asked with a laugh. He wandered to the door of the bathroom. "Nice clue as to what room you were in," he said as he smiled at her. "You look good in bubbles. If I had a camera with me I would take your picture. I guess I'll just have to commit this to memory. Too bad I can't see what's under all those bubbles," he chuckled.

"The night's young," she replied as she winked at him. "I was hoping you would understand my cryptic message. I'm so glad you did. Why don't you go open the bottle of champagne the hotel left and pour us a glass. I'll be out in a couple of minutes." She felt her heart start to race. She had fantasized about a night like this—a repeat of a wonderful memory from her past.

A CHANGED REFLECTION

"Wow, nice room. Must have set you back a pretty penny." She could hear the cork pop as she got out of the tub. "Champagne's a nice touch." He poured them each a glass.

"Not at all," she replied. "They just happened to oversell rooms this weekend and asked if I minded getting an upgrade for no extra charge. I couldn't say no."

She dried herself off and slipped into the black lace nightie and covered up with the black satin robe. She really didn't have a choice. It was the only thing she had in the bathroom. She ran her fingers through her hair. She spritzed herself with some perfume and brushed some gloss on her lips. She grabbed her phone as selections from her youth continued on Pandora.

His back was to her when she came into the room. He turned around. "Whoa. You look amazing," he said with a large grin settling on his face. She had forgotten how much taller he was than her. He handed her a glass of champagne. She set her phone down on the hall table.

She felt herself blushing. "Thanks. You looked pretty hot yourself in that suit of yours. Glad to see you got comfortable." She took the glass of champagne and smiled at him.

"I don't wear a suit much. Not really my style. Love what you're wearing now but you looked pretty hot in that dress of yours. The sparkles matched the sparkle in your eyes."

"Thank you. Come, sit down." Greg followed her to the sofa and they sat facing each other. "So shall we have a toast?" she asked him. She raised her glass and looked directly into his eyes and waited for his toast.

"Sure," he said with a grin as he put his hand on her thigh. "To Groundhog day," as he clinked his glass against hers. She suddenly felt goose bumps all over. Groundhog Day. His response when she had asked him, if given the chance, would he repeat that night they had spent together so many years before?

She had thought about that night over and over. The chemistry between them had been electric. Her heart was beating out of her chest. She slowly sipped her champagne and then set her glass down.

She grabbed the bottle of lotion that was on the table. "Do you mind?" she asked, as she removed the lid from the bottle.

"Not at all." He grinned. I'll just sit here and watch." She smiled. He had always told her she was a tease. No time like the present to toy with him. She squeezed the lotion into her palms and then very slowly started to massage the lotion onto her legs, starting with her feet. She methodically worked her way up her legs and very slowly and deliberately worked in the remainder of the lotion at the top of her thighs. The robe had fallen slightly open and he could see she wasn't wearing any panties.

"Dance with me. This is our song." He smiled. He grabbed her hand and pulled her off the sofa. "We danced to this song that night at the club." Bread was playing "Make It with You." He pulled her close. She could tell she had aroused him. She closed her eyes and enjoyed the warmth of his body against hers. She rested her head on his shoulder and stroked the back of his neck with her fingers.

She smiled as she listened to the words of the song. How she wished the moment would never end. It felt so good to be in his arms. She felt his hand slide slowly down to her ass as his fingers outlined the curves of her body. The moment brought back memories. Almost as if she were that young girl again, dancing at the club.

The song faded away and he very gently took her face in his hands and bent down and kissed her softly. She found herself standing on her tippy toes and kissing him back. When the kiss finally ended he pulled away slightly so he could look at her. "You're still beautiful, Tess. The years have been good to you."

"Thank you. I'm glad you think so, Greg," she replied. She pulled herself away. It was an automatic reaction when things became too intense. She turned and walked over to the table and picked up their champagne glasses. "I think you should pour us another glass. No need to waste it." She smiled.

He grabbed the glasses from her hands and poured them another glass. He gazed at her as they each took a sip. He took the glass from her hand and set both glasses down on the hall table. He grabbed her from behind and wrapped his arms around her. She felt happy in his arms. She wrapped her hands over his. She looked at their reflections in the mirror. "I'm not that twenty-year-old girl anymore."

He hugged her tight and then slid his hand over to the tie of her robe. "I'm not that twenty-year-old boy either," he whispered as he kissed her softly behind her ear. She giggled, and he felt her muscles tighten. "Still ticklish, I see," he laughed. "Relax." He pulled the tie and the robe fell open. He could see the black lace nightie that covered the curves of her body.

"You're beautiful and your breasts are still gorgeous." He continued to nibble at her ears and neck. She shrugged her shoulder on the side he was kissing. He nuzzled his face in and pushed her head back. He ran his lips up the side of her neck. He felt her body shiver. He gently pushed the robe from her shoulders. "Did you buy this little number for me?" he asked her with a smirk on his face.

"How did I know it would be you?" she said with an impish grin. "Do you like it?"

He stopped kissing her neck and looked at her reflection in the mirror. "Oh yeah." She smiled back at him. His hands slowly caressed her shoulders and then he leaned over and kissed them softly. His hands wandered across the curves of her body. She watched him intently.

His hands crept underneath the lace and found their way to her breasts. He squeezed them gently. She felt him make little circles on her nipples until they stood at attention. She felt chills all over her body and shuddered. Her breathing was becoming uneven. He smiled. "You like that, don't you?" he whispered in her ear.

"Yes, I do," she whispered as she took in a long breath and exhaled deeply. His hands then slid along her sides. She found herself taking short little breaths.

She suddenly felt his hand slowly creeping up her inner thigh. She could feel his hand gently but forcefully push her legs apart to accommodate his hand. His fingertips touched all the curves inquisitively. He could feel her body tense. His finger slipped between the folds of her skin and felt the wetness. She quietly gasped and took a deep breath in. "Breathe," he told her as kissed her neck. She exhaled and he laughed.

He stopped and turned her around. His hand stroked her face and he leaned over and kissed her long and hard. "I think this would be better," he said as he slipped the straps off her shoulders and pulled the nightie down until it fell to the floor. He pulled her close and rubbed his hands across her bare back while he kissed her neck.

He then turned her around so she was facing the mirror again. He squeezed her tightly in his arms. She wrapped her arms around his. "Very nice," he whispered in her ear. She was now totally naked in front of the mirror.

She watched in the mirror as he cupped each breast in his hands. Slowly he started rolling her nipples between his fingers. She smiled and reached one hand behind her. She gently ran her fingers through his hair. "Mmmmm," she cooed. He slowly slid one hand lower against her skin. He stopped for a moment and searched her eyes in the mirror. She looked back at him and smiled. He continued to fondle her breast with one hand but the other hand slowly slipped between her legs.

She was mesmerized by the reflection in the mirror. She had never watched in a mirror while anyone had touched her. She put both her hands around his neck, totally opening herself up to him. She watched as he slowly continued to explore the curves of her body. She was totally exposed to him. He kissed both sides of her neck and she whimpered.

He grinned. One hand found its way back to her breast and started to tease her nipple and massage her. The other hand slipped back between her legs and his finger slowly forced its way inside her, exploring. She moved to encompass his hand. She watched for a moment as her body filled with goose bumps. She reached for his hand and repositioned it until it made her gasp.

"Little circles, slowly," she whispered. Then she closed her eyes and took in the pleasure he was giving her. Her body started to clench.

"Open your eyes and watch," he commanded softly in her ear and smiled. "It's a beautiful sight."

She opened her eyes and watched the reflection in the mirror. Her body convulsed under his touch. When she could not tolerate the intensity any longer, she moved slightly. She stared at the woman in the mirror. No longer that reflection she had written about so many years before. She smiled as she tried to catch her breath.

She took her other hand from his neck, gently grabbed his arms and pulled away slightly so she could turn around. "I think someone else needs to lose a few clothes," she said breathlessly with a large grin. She grabbed his shirt and pulled him close. She looked up at him, and he smiled and kissed her gently on the lips. She started slowly unbuttoning his shirt. As each button was undone, Tess pulled his shirt open further and nuzzled her face into his sun kissed chest.

She tugged at the sleeves and pulled his shirt off. "Hold me close," she whispered. She loved the way her breasts felt against his bare skin. He smelled amazing. "You feel good," she said as her fingers caressed his neck. She took a deep breath and closed her eyes. She knew she needed to create a memory.

He grabbed her tighter and pressed her body closer to his. His hand slipped down and behind her and grabbed her ass and squeezed. She pulled away slightly and looked up at him. "I couldn't believe you did that in the elevator," she scolded.

"I wanted to see if you could keep your composure while I was touching you." He laughed.

She started to kiss his chest again and ran her fingers down his sides. When her fingers reached the top of his pants she very slowly and deliberately ran them across his torso until she had reached his belt buckle. She slowly unbuckled the belt. Then very carefully she unzipped the zipper. She reached behind his back and slid her hands into his pants and onto his ass and cradled it for a moment. Then very slowly she inched his jeans down. She kneeled down and helped him step out of them.

Then, without qualms or hesitation, she ran her fingers up the inner sides of his legs and kissed him along the way. He watched as she gently cradled his balls in her hands and then took him in her mouth, moving slowly in and out. She used her tongue to make swirling motions as she continued to move in and out. She circled the tip with her tongue and then stopped and looked up at him. "Do you like this?" She smiled.

"Oh yeah." She knew it was a question that didn't need to be asked but she had anyway. She knew she had the control over him as she held him in her mouth.

She continued until she felt his body was almost ready to explode and then applied gentle pressure. "Not yet," she whispered. She slowly slid her body up against his and wrapped her arms around him and pulled him close. She loved the feel of his hardness against her. He pulled away slightly and grabbed her hand and led her into the bedroom.

"So tell me your fantasy," he said as he sat down on the edge of the bed and pulled her close as he nuzzled his face in her breasts and kissed them gently.

"My fantasy is to have a lot of hot, sweaty sex with someone who wants it, really wants me," she replied. "Someone who makes my heart skip a beat." He nuzzled her breasts and kissed them tenderly.

"Like me?" he asked looking into her eyes.

She smiled. "Like you," she said as she stroked his face and looked intently back into his eyes. "What about you?" she asked.

"I want to see you lying totally naked on the bed, just like I did before." He scooped her up in his arms and laid her gently onto the bed. "You're still just as beautiful as I remember." He smiled. He lay down next to her, brushing the hair out of her eyes and kissed her long and hard. Her body tingled. Her nipples were erect. His closeness took her breath away.

He gazed at her and carefully ran his hands and lips across her body as if he was discovering a treasure. She closed her eyes and concentrated on the sensation his hands and kisses were creating on her skin. Slow, deliberate touches meant to elicit a reaction. First her nipples and then his hand followed the curves of her body until he found his way between her legs. She found her breathing becoming rapid again. He watched her and smiled.

She leaned close to him, stroked his face and whispered in his ear, "In my bag beside the bed is some massage oil. I'd love you to rub it all over me." He leaned over the side of the bed and opened the bag.

"Your wish is my command," he replied with a smile. "I see you brought your toys with you."

She grinned. "I don't need them tonight, I have you," she said quietly as she nibbled on his ear.

"The real thing is always better." She took his face in her hands and kissed him passionately as if it were their last kiss, creating a memory. He drew her close and kissed her back with the same intensity.

He took the oil, poured some into his hands and warmed it before massaging it slowly into her neck, across her breasts and then down the sides of her body. Then he started at her feet and worked his way up her legs and onto her inner thighs. "Mmmmmm," she started to coo.

He stopped and smiled. "From the sounds you're making, I'm assuming you're enjoying yourself."

She looked at him and smiled. "More than you know," she whispered.

He continued rubbing until her body trembled under his touch. Then he slowly moved his finger and pushed it inside her. She let out a little gasp. He smiled and continued to move his finger in and out. He felt her lift her body to meet his finger. He stopped and she stroked his face and smiled.

She took his hand and guided it back between her legs. "Middle finger," she quietly directed him as he slipped it back inside her. "Now curve it upward," she instructed. He started to explore and could tell by her body's reaction when he had found the spot. He used his thumb at the same time to massage her until he felt her body tighten and then shudder. He delighted in the vision he was creating.

She was breathing hard. He finally stopped and smiled at her. He cupped her breasts in his hands and kissed them tenderly. "Still the gold standard in my book." He knew she had enjoyed herself. She looked intently at him. Her breathing was becoming more regular again. She had an impish look in her eyes. "What's going on in that pretty little head of yours?"

She grinned and pushed him onto his back. She poured some massage oil into her hand and straddled him. She looked him directly in his eyes and took him in her hand and moved it up and down applying gentle pressure. She rubbed the end in her fingertips. She took him in her mouth for a few moments and then kissed his balls before she continued to kiss his body as she slowly slid her body up across his and whispered into his ear, "Tell me you want me."

"You know I do, Tess." She straddled him and used her hand to guide him in. She let out a gasp as he entered her. He cradled her breasts as she continued the rhythmic thrusting. He smiled as he watched her lose herself in pleasure.

"Come in me. I want to feel your warmth inside of me," she whispered. He grabbed her hips and thrust deeply into her. She knew he was close. The ebb and flow lasted only a few moments before she felt him come inside her as her body tightened in a spasm. She smiled as she tried to catch her breath. She lay down on top of him, kissed him gently, and snuggled in close. She felt content for the first time in a very long time. "Hold me close for a while," she pleaded.

"As long as you want, Tess," he replied. They lay together in each other's embrace for what seemed like hours.

He finally brushed the hair out of her eyes and looked deep into her eyes. "Was it worth waiting for?" he asked her. She looked directly back into his eyes, searching his soul.

"It's a perfect memory," she whispered and smiled.

Chapter Twenty-Three

Tess woke to a clap of thunder followed by the gentle patter of rain. She loved the sound of rain on the roof at the lake. The rain was causing the acorns to tumble down at an alarming rate. She rolled over and fell back into a restless sleep. When she woke up again, the rain had stopped, but it was still dismal outside. The weather fit her mood. She hated that the time had come to say good-bye to the lake house for the season. This time it was even more painful. How she wished Cat was there to bounce things off.

She dragged herself out of bed. She walked down the hall and stopped to look out across the lake. Even with the dreary day, the lake was beautiful. Calming. She wondered if her MEME had felt the same feelings when she had looked at water. Had she felt the same sadness when she left the island?

She knew what she needed to do, but she was dreading every second of it. The lake was her happy place, and closing it for the winter made her extremely sad. She returned to her room and grabbed her sweats that were thrown on the chair and slipped them on. It didn't matter what she looked like today. An overwhelming ache filled her heart. She was missing her mother.

Tess decided she would wait to see if the weather improved slightly before doing her outside chores. She headed down the steps slowly, as if that might somehow prolong the inevitable. "Someday, Mom," she said out loud to herself, "I won't have to leave here. This is where I belong. This is home."

She picked up the TV remote and clicked the TV on and then scrolled through the channels until she reached the music channels.

She decided on a nostalgic one. Different thoughts of the past had filled her mind since that night with him and had left her wondering. Good and bad memories. *Might as well be totally in the moment*, she thought. Music made all things bearable in her life. Music had the ability to cut to the core and significantly alter her mood and spirit. She knew her world would be empty without it. Music and writing. She had started to journal again. It felt good. Words were her therapy. She knew they would help her find her way.

    She cranked the volume so that she could hear the music from the kitchen. She grabbed the kettle and filled it. It was a good morning for some tea. She would let the kettle go until it screamed out how it felt inside. She understood that feeling. It was creeping into her life more and more. She knew she had to deal with it. Words Greg had said left her wondering, and life with Michael was becoming unbearable. She knew Cat was right. She opened the pantry door and grabbed a tea bag and set it inside her tea cup.

    Tess looked back into the pantry, shook her head, and sighed. Too much stuff. How did everything around her seem to get filled with too much stuff that suddenly seemed to have no purpose? Just like the pantry, relationships in her life needed to be sorted out, separated into appropriate memories, stored away, or tossed. Some memories would be allowed to stay while she created new ones. Some needed to be tossed even though it would be painful. Others would need to be packed neatly away. Accessible only on rare occasions. Her heart needed to be ready for what a new spring would bring.

    She pulled up the step stool and sat down on it in front of the pantry. Cleaning and sorting out the pantry was always an arduous task each fall. She grabbed the first box of opened crackers. Even though in her mind she knew they would need to be tossed, she had to try one just in case. "Really?" she said out loud to herself as she spit the cracker out. They no longer had their crispness and were not even worth dealing with. They belonged in the circular file as did all the other boxes and bags that had been opened at the beginning of summer. That part was easy. If only sorting through the memories were that easy.

A CHANGED REFLECTION

Tess smiled. Yes, she realized that some relationships were exactly like the box of crackers. Some of the boxes were right on the edge. Almost worth keeping, but was it really worth the effort or time to salvage them? The teakettle whistled, and she poured the hot water into the cup to steep.

Next she checked for all the things that had somehow retreated to the back recesses of the cupboard and had become outdated. They too belonged in the circular file. Tess knew there were feelings and memories that had retreated to the back recesses of her mind. She needed to deal with them once and for all. Memories, good and bad, needed to find their place. The things that would last until the spring were placed in a basket. When she was finished cleaning, she would carry the basket to the basement for the winter.

Time for tea. She grabbed the cup and went to the dining room. She sat down at the dining room table in the chair her mother had always sat in. The chair that had somehow become her chair. She slowly sipped her tea, letting the liquid warm her body and soul. She closed her eyes and remembered the warmth she had felt in his arms. A wonderful memory, yet her intuition told her that perhaps this was one of those memories that should be stored in a special place in her heart and remembered.

She continued slowly sipping her tea until it was gone. She took her cup into the kitchen and placed it in the sink and headed to the spa room. She grabbed the bag of mismatched plastic containers that somehow had all lost their lids. She frowned as she looked at them. How did all those lids just disappear? It was like the socks in the dryer. Someday they would all resurface, only by then the bottoms of the containers and the mate to each sock would be long gone. Perhaps resurfaced memories had come too late.

She picked up the bag of hedge apples she had collected and started to distribute them between the containers. She smiled as she thought about the funny looks she had gotten when she had stopped at the park after dark to pick them up. She guessed it wasn't the usual thing the late-night dog walkers saw. Hedge apples seemed to keep the spiders away. It had worked before during the previous winter, so she was willing to try it again. It was better than bombing the house with bug spray.

She sorted the apples and placed the appropriate sizes into the containers that would hold them. Now it was time to distribute them to the nooks and crannies of the house. As she delivered a container to the last bedroom, she noticed that the sun was trying to emerge from behind the clouds. It might turn out to be a nice day after all. If she worked quickly, she might be able to get one last glimpse of a sunset. A beautiful sunset put all things in perspective.

She returned to the kitchen and looked at the basket from the pantry that was to go to the basement. By spring would she really even use these things? Was it like her life? She kept holding on to things because it was easier to "store" them than to deal with them? Cat's words echoed in her head. "Tess, all the markers are there. It's time." She picked up the basket and took it to the basement. Like so many other things, she would store it for a while.

She rummaged around the basement and found the pump and hose so she could empty the hot tub. She frowned. It was by far the most distasteful project in the closing of the house. The hot tub was a place of great stress release for her. She had often wished she had one at her home in the city.

She closed her eyes and listened to the sucking hum of the pump as the water spewed out into the sink through the kitchen window. She had perfected a way to keep the hose in the sink without spraying all over. She was like her mother in that respect. Always fiddling and fidgeting with things to make things easier or better. Sometimes it became a challenge. She smiled. She and her cousin Cat were always partaking in "challenges."

The change in the sound of the hum made her realize that the tub was almost empty and she would have to manually remove the rest of the water. She had yet to figure out how to automate that process. Once she had sponged away the last traces of remaining water, she climbed out of the hot tub and set her bucket down. Time to head outdoors.

She ventured to the shed to get a yard waste disposal sack. She began pulling the dead flowers from the window boxes and filling the sack. Each spring she would plant the tiny flowers, and they would barely show above the tops of the window boxes. By the end of the summer, they were plush and full and beautiful. Then the frost would come along and kill them, and they would turn into a droopy mess.

Box by box she cleared away the mess. The ones on the first story were so much easier to deal with than those on the second floor. She would need to do this with her past and present if she were to be able to move freely into her future. Just like the flower boxes, some parts of her life would be harder to deal with. The sack remained half-full, or was it half-empty?

She returned to the shed and grabbed a rake. She racked up the leaves by the doors and threw them into the sack. It filled the sack, and she set it by the curb for the garbage men to take away. She continued racking and filling sacks until her ADHD set in. She raked the remaining leaves from the middle of the yard next to the street and hoped the wind would blow them away. It wouldn't be long before she would be returning to scoop the snow away from the doors. She sighed.

A chill filled the air. Tess had worked up a sweat, and the breeze caused her to shiver. She headed to the lake to grab the furniture from the alcove to put it away for the winter. It took her three trips to get everything, but it fit nicely into the guesthouse. She noticed the sun was getting lower in the sky. Fall was in the air, and she decided it was time to go back inside and make herself another cup of tea.

Tess made sure her tea was extra hot before she sat down at the dining room table. She knew her life had suddenly become very complicated. It was as if a key had unlocked a door that had been closed for a very long time. Feelings that had been locked away had once again resurfaced. There was no way to go back. She knew even if she could, she didn't want to. Things had changed. She had changed.

She gazed out the windows toward the lake. The setting sun created a beautiful canvas across the sky. The remaining leaves were falling like a gentle rain. The lake was smooth as glass without a boat on it. Picture perfect.

Perfect. Just like that weekend had been. The mind replays what the heart can't delete. Tess had played it over and over in her mind.

It was another memory etched into her soul. Her heart could not delete it, nor did she even want to try. She had the memory that no one could take away.

But it was the end of the summer, and perhaps it was time to say good-bye. Maybe good-bye to everything. Another spring would come, and things would begin anew. As much as she had loved the summer and every moment she had spent with Greg, it had left a nagging feeling behind. Something just didn't add up. And she knew she had to make drastic changes in her own life.

She got up from the table and picked up her cup to take it to the kitchen. She caught her reflection in the mirror. She set her cup down on the buffet and stopped to study it. There was something very different about it now.

It was not the young girl who had looked back at her while sitting at the vanity brushing her long golden-brown hair in high school with tears in her eyes. It was not the confused bride who had looked at herself on the day of her wedding and wondered if she was doing the right thing. It was not the woman she had seen in the mirror at the beginning of the summer. It was not even the woman who had been told to open her eyes only a few short weeks ago on that magical night.

She had really opened her eyes. There had been a wonderful and amazing transformation. You could see it in her face. It was a changed reflection. She looked intently at the reflection. True happiness, acceptance, contentment. Finally understanding her past. She liked the face looking back at her.

About the Author

Ashley Wylder is from the Midwest where she was raised on a farm in North Central Iowa. Her childhood was a happy one. After graduating from high school and college, she never settled more than two hours from that home.

Ashley struggled in her adolescent years as many young girls do. Decisions made in her youth had long lasting consequences. She spent years trying to find her passion in life and who she really was.

She now lives in her family's lake home in Northern Iowa. It was that happy place where her inspiration took wings.